MISTER RURAL DEAN

Mister
Rural Dean

FRED SECOMBE

HarperCollins*Publishers*

HarperCollins*Publishers*
77–85 Fulham Palace Road, London W6 8JB

First published in Great Britain in 1999 by HarperCollins*Publishers*

Copyright © 1999 Fred Secombe

1 3 5 7 9 10 8 6 4 2

Fred Secombe asserts the moral right to be
identified as the author of this work

A catalogue record for this book is
available from the British Library

ISBN 0 00 628118 4

Printed and bound in Great Britain by
Creative Print and Design (Wales), Ebbw Vale

'Of all the terrors known to man, the greatest, I assert, is to wear a fifteen collar upon a sixteen shirt,' I gasped, as I tried to fasten the collar of a major-general around the neck of my Curate.

'Is that in the *Oxford Book of English Verse?*' he enquired.

'Nothing so exalted,' I replied. 'It comes from the middle page of the *Daily Express* under the heading of "Beachcomber". I wish to heaven that you were not so given to sporting activities, then perhaps your neck would not be quite so thick.'

'From what I can see of this military headdress,' he said, 'it looks as if the same adjective could be applied to my head.'

'Hugh Thomas,' I murmured, 'is it only now that you have come to realize that?'

'Vicar!' he expostulated.

It was the dress rehearsal of the Abergelly Church Gilbert and Sullivan Society's production of *The Pirates of Penzance* in the local Miners' Welfare Hall. I had formed the company some ten months earlier, my second venture into the realm of the Savoy opera. This was another Pooh-Bah excuse for me, since I was the producer, director and principal tenor, while Mrs Pooh-Bah was the principal soprano, choreographer and wardrobe mistress: the Secombes Limited.

The dressing rooms were in a state of chaos. My wife had already inspected the home-made costumes of the pirates at the previous rehearsal – dark trousers, wellingtons, rugby jerseys and head scarves. They had drawn the line at wearing earrings. To our great consternation, the baskets from the costumier had been late arriving. It was four o'clock when they made their appearance at the hall. In the men's dressing room there was a scrum around the baskets as I attempted to allocate the costumes. Apart from a few cases of severe constriction such as my Curate's uniform, the majority of those cast as police pronounced themselves to be well satisfied with their outfits. The only exception, apart from a few obese members of the chorus, was Ivor Hodges, my churchwarden, who had a beanpole of a figure. As the sergeant of police, the tunic amply covering his bony presence was held in place with a large belt, fastened to its ultimate notch, giving the impression that he was wearing a blouse. Hugh Thomas had managed to ram his head into the plumed helmet of the Major-General – perhaps 'part of his head' would be a better description. I felt that if he raised his eyebrows too often, sooner or later his helmet would shoot off like a rocket.

In the ladies' dressing room, my wife, Eleanor, had a more difficult task, coping with young ladies, all of whom aspired to be decorative on stage. Almost all of them were pleased with their Victorian dresses. However, three of the more corpulent suffered from the same constraint as the overweight policemen. The spokeswoman for the trio, Myfanwy Morgan, a sixteen-year-old with vital statistics which belied her age, suggested that my wife had taken the wrong measurements. 'We was among the last when you did us and you was in a hurry, if you remember.'

'My dear Myfanwy,' my wife replied, 'it is more than six weeks since the forms were sent to the costumier. It is quite possible that you have put on weight in that time. If I am not mistaken, you were finishing off a packet of fish and chips outside the hall when I came in this evening. As a doctor I would advise you to avoid such food for the rest of this week and it may be that your costume will be more comfortable by the end of the show.' There were no more complaints.

Meanwhile in the hall, Graham Webb, the musical director, who was on the staff of Ivor Hodges, the head-master of the local secondary modern school, was attempting to weld fourteen instrumentalists, recruited from various places in the valleys, into an orchestra. From what I could hear coming through the open door of the dressing room, the conductor was rivalling Sir Thomas Beecham at his loudest and most uncomplimentary in rehearsal.

'If he carries on like that,' said my Curate, 'we shall be performing to a piano accompaniment.'

'I'm afraid he thinks he is in the school hall,' said Ivor Hodges. 'That sort of attitude works there but this is the Miners' Welfare Hall. He will soon find out the difference. Still, he is an excellent musician and that may be sufficient to prevent a walkout.'

I had been Vicar of Abergelly for more than three years, a large industrial parish in the West Monmouthshire valleys. They were years of toil and tribulation as I strove to cope with thirty years of neglect by my predecessor. By now my wife and I had settled down with our young children, David and Elspeth, in the Vicarage in the centre of the town. Eleanor had established a practice in the newly built housing estate of Brynfelin, spreadeagled on the hill above Abergelly, where I had erected a prefabricated building to serve as a church. We were enabled to live our busy lives by having an excellent housekeeper, Mrs Cooper, who provided us with splendid food and an endless supply of malapropisms to lighten our burdens. The other escape route from the demands upon us was our mutual love of Gilbert and Sullivan. For ten months of the year we could leave our worries behind us and relax with the delightful music of Sir Arthur Sullivan and the wit of W.S. Gilbert. I salved my conscience about the time I spent in indulging my passion for G and S by the thought, that as in my last parish, some of the members of the society appeared in my confirmation classes. As my wife said, 'It is all part of your outreach, my love, evangelism by stealth, as it were.'

The local hairdresser, Simeon Jones, had volunteered his services as a make-up artist in the men's dressing room. A dapper little man sporting an auburn wig and a waxed grey moustache with auburn tinges produced by tobacco, he told me that he was a thespian of many years' standing. 'Too old to tread the boards now,' he said, 'but I'm only too pleased to be a backroom boy.'

Most of the male chorus were members of the Abergelly Male Voice Choir, to whom greasepaint was a novelty. They formed a disorderly, vociferous queue as they waited to receive Simeon's attention. 'Better keep that on to go home, Will,' said one of them to the first to arrive from the barber's chair. 'It'll do wonders for your love life. Your missus won't recognize you.'

Waiting impatiently in the chorus line was Willie James, the Scoutmaster of the church troop. Barely five foot in height, he had come to the first rehearsal clutching a score of *The Pirates of Penzance* and announcing that he wished to be auditioned for the part of the Pirate King. Earlier in the evening, he had asked me if he could keep his glasses on. 'I can't see a thing without them, Vicar,' he said.

'My dear Willie, either you keep them off or else you keep them on and sing from behind the scenery.'

He replied he would 'take a chance' and 'have a go' without them.

Overhearing this conversation, Dai Elbow, six foot tall and fourteen stone in weight, suggested that it would be better for the production if he kept his specs on. Dai was a former back-row forward in the Abergelly rugby team, who had earned his title by the illegal use of his elbow in rugby matches and ended up by being banned for life from the game. Off the field, he was a most congenial person and was one of my right-hand men in the parish. Already he had spent most of the day in helping the stage manager to erect the scenery. The stage manager was Tom Beynon, the people's warden, a short stocky man who was nearing his retirement as a miner in the local colliery. Tom had no previous experience as a stage manager but he was a born organizer and an ideal handyman. Over the last week he had learned a lot from Peter Henderson, who was the art master at Ivor Hodges' school.

Peter had painted the scenery for the production. It was a delightful representation of what the D'Oyly Carte production copy described as 'a rocky seashore on the Cornish coast'. The stage at the Miners' Welfare was most commodious and its backcloth had featured in many musical comedy productions. Peter's work of art ranked with the best of them.

Since there was no change of scenery in the interval, it meant that Tom's introduction into stage management was a painless exercise. He found the erection of the flats with the assistance of Dai Elbow was a straightforward operation. Already he was looking forward to a more challenging proposition when the society had to provide a change of scenery after Act 1. 'I can see me at the London Palladium when I retire,' he told me.

Graham Webb was still engaged in a contretemps with the woodwind section of the orchestra when I entered the hall. Anita Jones, the flautist with an Eton crop and a long top lip, was complaining about the speed on which he was insisting during a passage in the finale of Act 1. 'We are not the Hallé orchestra,' she said indignantly.

Before he could reply, I shouted, 'We are ready, Graham.' Red-faced, he swallowed a retort, tapped his music stand with a petulant swipe of his baton and, through gritted teeth, instructed the players to turn to the overture.

Behind the curtain the pirates were getting into position for the opening chorus. There was as much excitement as there would be in Cardiff Arms Park prior to the kick-off in an international against England. As I moved to take my seat at the back of the stage, the orchestra began the overture. There was an instant hush. Bryn Matthews, the short fat baritone of the male voice chorus who had been cast as Samuel and had the opening solo, stood frozen with fright, holding a big jug which showed the only sign of movement on stage as it wobbled in his trembling hand. I left my place as Frederic beside Ruth, the Pirate Maid of all Work, and strode into the centre.

'Come on, boyos,' I said, like a master addressing his pupils. 'Let's keep the excitement going, and don't forget, I want plenty of laughter and a good cheer given to Samuel when he appears with fresh flagons of wine.' It had the desired effect. By the time the curtain went up there was a loud greeting for Samuel followed by a spirited rendering of 'Pour, oh pour the pirate sherry'.

Far from encouraging Bryn Matthews, this appeared to unnerve him still further. The opening lines of his solo, sung pianissimo instead of bel canto, should have registered as 'For today our pirate 'prentice rises from indenture freed'. This emerged as 'For today our pirate dentist rises from his dentures freed'. As it was, he was only audible on stage. An audience would have been incapable of hearing him against the background of the orchestra.

Between his two short solo items, he was required to perform a 'clumsy' dance. Totally devoid of balletic skills, Bryn found a step and a hop in tune to the music an impossible exercise. In rehearsal he had attempted what was the clumsiest of dances. Now he abandoned all pretence of primitive ballet and contented himself with going around the groups of pirates, tipping up the empty jug to fill the empty tankards and mugs, ending with one hop as the chorus finished.

By now the chorus had entered into the spirit of the opera and were laughing and shouting as they indulged in their mimed drinking. With the arrival of Gareth Morgan as the Pirate King, a big commanding figure, the scene came alive. By the time he began his solo, 'Oh better far to live and die under the brave black flag I fly', it was obvious that the show would be a success. The entry of the chorus of girls, climbing over the rocky mountains, was a well-rehearsed piece of choreography and was applauded by the handful of voluntary helpers in the front row. The Curate's performance of the tongue-twisting solo which announced the appearance of the Major-General was impeccable, while the singing of the whole company in the unaccompanied chorus 'Hail Poetry' was the highlight of the finale of Act 1. 'That was beautiful,' pronounced Tom Beynon.

In the interval, while half of the pirates were being transformed into the squad of policemen, Bryn Matthews came up and apologized for his debacle in the opening scene.

'I suppose it might have been stage fright,' he said. 'Tomorrow I'm going to have a drop of the 'ow's your father before I go on the stage.'

'For heaven's sake, Bryn, don't do that!' I replied. 'When we did *Pirates* in Pontywen the man playing the Pirate King suffered like you at the dress rehearsal and decided to resort to the whisky bottle. By the time he was ready to leave home for the first night he was in such a state that he mistook the barometer in the hall for a clock and told his wife that he was late for the show. It took several cups of black coffee to sober him up.'

'I expect you're right, Vicar,' he said. 'I don't drink that much, and if I overdid it I'd make an even bigger fool of myself than I did tonight. In any case, by the time the first act ended I felt much more at ease.'

Eleanor came into the dressing room with a cushion. 'Ivor!' she shouted over the hubbub. 'Here's your corporation.' Then she turned to me. 'You fix him up, Fred, I've got to get back to the girls.'

When I had inserted the cushion in his tunic, the Sergeant of the Police became an imposing reality. Willie James came up to me, his diminutive figure swamped by a police uniform. 'This isn't a good fit, Vicar,' he complained.

'Willie,' I said, 'it's perfect. You are the comic policeman at the end of the line. The more bizarre you look, the better.'

His reaction to my words was immediate. 'I didn't realize I was the comic,' he said, as if he had been given an accolade.

I should never have said it. As soon as he made his entrance, he adopted a bandy-legged gait. He came out of line repeatedly, deliberately dropping his truncheon, and when eventually the policemen marched off the stage he turned around and waved goodbye with his truncheon.

The only other incident of note occurred when Hugh Thomas came on as the Major-General in dressing gown and nightcap. In his solo 'Sighing softly to the river' he had to run with little steps and then pose, listening with his hand to his ear. After three little steps, Simeon Jones' handiwork came apart and half of his moustache fell off.

My Curate made the most of this failure of the spirit gum by stooping down, picking up the detached half and spitting on it, then holding it to his upper lip with his left hand and gesturing with his right hand. All the while he was prancing about the stage and singing his lines as if nothing had happened. This manoeuvre produced laughter from the members of the orchestra, which annoyed the musical director who tapped the music stand and halted the music.

'Please keep your eyes on the music and not on the stage. Let's be professional, shall we?' he snapped.

'In that case,' announced my Curate, 'hold on until I get some running repairs to my whiskers.' He ran off to his dressing room with the detached half of the moustache. I followed him in.

'It wouldn't be a bad idea if I did this every night this week,' he said.

'Oh no you don't!' I replied. 'As Graham Webb told his orchestra, let's be professional.'

Simeon Jones was sitting down reading the evening paper. 'Quick!' said my Curate, 'half of my moustache has become unstuck.'

'You must have been playing about with it,' said the hairdresser. 'My moustaches never come off.'

'Excuse me!' expostulated Hugh. 'I never touched it. You are all right, *your* moustache is permanently fixed – evidently mine was not.'

Simeon went to his bottle of spirit gum and his brush. Then he grasped the Major-General's face with a vice-like grip and pressed the false hair to the upper lip with such force that it might have been a flat iron at work. 'Now then,' he breathed, 'try and pull that one off.'

'If I did,' Hugh replied belligerently, 'I think my head would come off with it.'

Back in the Vicarage, Eleanor and I relaxed on the settee and reviewed the dress rehearsal. 'Let's face it,' she said, 'it was a bit of a shambles – if anything, worse than the one at Pontywen. I must have those girls on the stage tomorrow night before the curtain goes up, for a rehearsal of their entrance. I think I shall hold back Myfanwy Morgan and her two fellow carthorses until the others have completed the dance. They can come on unobtrusively, I hope, and move into place in the chorus.'

'Apart from those three,' I replied, 'I think the girls were quite good. My headache is Willie James. As a pirate, his loud voice and his phoney Cornish accent stick out like a sore thumb from behind the curtains at the opening. As a police constable, his Charlie Chaplin act is ruining their entrance. I shall have some firm words to say to him, but I am afraid he is so carried away by the thrill of being on stage that he will forget anything I have told him and just let himself go.'

'Well, my dear,' my wife remarked, 'at least he will be funny, and you can't say that about Myfanwy and Co.'

We both agreed that the principals had given a satisfactory account of themselves. Elizabeth Williams, as Ruth, in voice and in acting was an impressive performer, as was Gareth Morgan as the Pirate King, with his gravelly tones and his commanding presence. Ivor Hodges as the Sergeant of Police was more conscious of the cushion stuck inside his tunic than he was of his persona as a fat policeman.

'To be fair to him,' said Eleanor, 'he had very little

time to get used to his corpulence. However, your Curate revelled in his promotion to the rank of Major-General.'

'I am afraid,' I explained, 'that he comes into the category of Willie James, somewhat OTT. I'll have a word with him after Matins tomorrow.'

'If I may say so,' she said quietly, 'your other persona could have been similarly classified by your reaction to the entry of the young ladies upon your stretch of seashore.'

'I beg your pardon!' I replied, with more than a hint of high dudgeon. 'I have to describe them as "blushing buds of ever-blooming beauty".'

'That does not mean as the front line of the chorus of the Folies Bergère,' came the riposte. On that note of disharmony, we went to bed.

Next day, Tuesday, was the appointed time for the monthly administration of the sick Communions. The Curate was responsible for those on the Brynfelin estate, where he was in charge of the 'prefab' daughter church. When we met at Matins, Hugh Thomas asked if he might be allowed to switch his duties to the following day. 'Janet has the bonus of a day off due to her and we thought to go to Cardiff to do some shopping.'

Janet Rees was his fiancée and the organist at St David's. A contralto with a pleasing but not very powerful voice, she had the part of Kate in *Pirates*. The two of them were inseparable. At rehearsals they took every opportunity to be together.

'For heaven's sake, Hugh,' I said, 'don't forget to be back in plenty of time for our first night. My wife wants the girls to be early to go through their first entrance and you will need to be early to make sure that our make-up artist makes a better job of your moustache. By the way, you were very good last night, but stick to what we have rehearsed. Don't go altering the script and the routine. For example, in your patter song you ended your first verse with the "whatsit" instead of the "square" of the hypotenuse.'

'Sorry, Vicar, but I had forgotten the word,' he replied. 'It will be "square" tonight.'

'Are you going by train or by your ancient machine?' I asked.

'Vicar!' he exploded. 'How can you refer to my vintage MG in such a way? I have had it serviced and it is in perfect condition to convey us to Cardiff. It will be much more reliable than the valleys railway timetable.'

When I went back to the Vicarage for my customary cup of coffee which accompanied my daily struggle with *The Times* crossword, I found a note on my desk from my wife who had left for her morning surgery at Brynfelin. 'The Rural Dean rang. (Evidently he doesn't have daily Matins.) He would like two tickets for Wednesday night for the Gilbert and Sullivan concert. I told him he could pick them up at the box office. Love, Mabel.'

The Reverend Llewellyn Evans, BA, RD, who thought in Welsh and translated it into mangled English, was quite unaware of what would happen at the Abergelly Miners' Welfare Hall. He had seen our advertisement in the local newspaper and, being a notorious busybody, had decided to investigate what the Vicar was doing off duty, as it were. Sitting at my desk I could imagine his surprise at seeing the Vicar and his wife, transformed into Frederic and Mabel, making musical love on the Cornish seashore. Add to that the shock of seeing the Curate cavorting around the stage as the comic, then the minor dignitary would be convinced the ecclesiastical world was standing on its head in Abergelly. Wednesday night could not come soon enough.

That morning I had to take Communion to Herbert Wilson, an insurance agent who was in the last stages of cancer of the lungs. I was not looking forward to my visit because poor Herbert had become a living skeleton. His face had shrunk into a skull and his bony arms would be uplifted to receive the sacrament. He had an eighteen-year-old daughter, a very pretty girl who doted on her father, and a devoted wife who waited on him with the utmost loving care. I sat outside the house in my car for some minutes before I could face the scene which awaited me. The invalid had been transferred to the front room of a semi-detached in a crescent of houses built in the 1930s. He was a Yorkshireman who had married an Abergelly girl whom he had met in the forces. He had told me that they had a large amount still to pay on their mortgage, and he was hoping he could get back to work to cope with his financial obligations.

Mrs Wilson opened the door to me and put her fingers to her lips. She led me past the front room and into the living room. There had not been the usual smile of greeting. Instead, once she had closed the door, she burst into tears. I put an arm around her to comfort her. As I did so, she stiffened up and pulled away from me.

'Sorry, Vicar,' she said. 'I must take control of myself. You see, the doctor came this morning. He told me that my husband has only a few more days to live at most. I mustn't be selfish in wanting him to hang on to such a God-awful existence.' The last few words were spoken with a bitter intensity. Then she went on, 'He is awake, and he is looking forward to having his Communion. If you don't mind, I'd like to take the sacrament with him. I know I'm not confirmed, but I'm sure God won't mind, will he? In any case, his voice is so weak now that he will need me to speak up for him. I've got the prayer book here. If you can show me the parts where I have to say my bit, that will be a help.'

She handed me the book which was on the table. It was in pristine condition.

'His mother gave it to him when he was confirmed. She was a good churchwoman. I am sure she would be pleased to know that his Baptist wife would be using it for his very last Communion. Perhaps it will make up for us getting married in Bethesda instead of St Peter's.'

By now she had recovered her composure. As we entered the front room, I was met with an all-pervading odour of disinfectant. Sitting propped up by his pillows was what was left of a human being after being eaten away by the malignant demons of cancer.

As I put out the chalice and paten on the immaculately clean lace tablecloth covering the top of the bedside cabinet, I said to Herbert, 'We are going to have a congregation this morning. Your dear wife will be another communicant.'

He looked at her and attempted a smile. 'Better late than never, love,' he breathed.

It was the most moving service I had ever conducted. Only by the grace of God was I able to control a rising tide of tears. When I gave them the blessing at the end of the administration, I understood what was meant by 'the peace of God which passeth all understanding'. He held her hand as the service ended, and they both remained with their eyes closed for several minutes.

Very quietly, with the coaster from the Toby jug I cleansed the vessels. Then I removed my surplice and stole, put the chalice and paten in their case and knelt by the bedside for a moment. As I straightened up, Herbert looked at me. 'Thank you, Vicar,' he murmured.

Edith Wilson stood up. 'I'll see you to the door,' she said quietly.

'See you next month, God willing,' I told the invalid.

'I hope he is,' he replied.

As she stood on the doorstep, she kissed me lightly on the cheek. 'You're a good man,' she said.

For the rest of the morning I was in a trance. Herbert Wilson's face confronted me in the car, at my desk and at the dinner table. 'What on earth is the matter with you?' asked Eleanor. 'You are just like a zombie. I hope you will come to life by tonight.'

'I should have postponed my sick Communions until next week,' I replied. 'I took the sacrament to Herbert Wilson this morning. Apparently he has only a few days to live. It was like administering to a skeleton. His face has haunted me ever since. I am in no mood to dress up and pretend to be a pirate.'

We were drinking coffee in the privacy of the sitting room while Mrs Cooper was washing up the dishes in the kitchen. Eleanor came across to me as I sat in an armchair. She perched herself on the arm and lifted my face gently.

Looking into my eyes, she said softly, 'My dear love, I have told you many a time that you would never make a doctor. The last thing that poor man would wish to do would be to put a damper on the proceedings at the Welfare Hall. I have a few home visits to do this afternoon, otherwise I would suggest that we drove into the countryside for an hour or so. Why don't you go across to Tom Beynon's and have a chat with your jovial churchwarden? Pretend that you have come to see that he has got everything in hand for tonight. You don't want to be mooching about on your own for the next couple of hours.' She kissed me and added, 'Go on, do as your doctor tells you, there's a good boy.' I did as I was told and walked down to Tom's house in Merthyr Street.

His wife, Winnie, opened the door to me. She was a small thin lady in her late fifties, with a shy smile and a strong preference for staying in the background. 'Come on in, Vicar,' she said. 'Tom has just finished his dinner after coming off his six to two shift. Go into the front room. I'll get him now.'

I sat down in the chintz-covered armchair in the bay window and gazed at the family photographs on the mantelpiece, the most prominent of which was Tom and Winnie's wedding group outside St Peter's. The strong smell of tobacco smoke heralded the appearance of the man of the house, clad in bracered trousers and open-necked flannel shirt.

'Excuse the outfit, Vicar,' said the churchwarden. 'I'm not prepared to receive visitors – but there, you don't come into that category, more of a friend of the family, isn't it?'

'I hope so, Tom,' I replied.

'Now, before we get down to the purpose of your call, what about a glass of stout?' he enquired.

'Fine,' I said.

He disappeared, puffing smoke from his pipe in clouds of obnoxious fumes and returning a few minutes later, carrying a tray containing two bottles and glasses, but minus his pipe. 'I've had a ticking-off from Winnie for smoking in the front room. Talk about the laws of the Medes and Persians, I say. By the way, what were those laws, Vicar?'

'I haven't the faintest idea, nowadays,' I replied. 'I might have known something about them when I was in college, but that was a long time ago.'

'Come off it, Vicar,' he said. 'You're only a baby. Anyway, what is it that you want to see me about?'

'To be honest, Tom, I was going to ask you if you've got everything in hand as far as the stage is concerned for tonight. But that's not the real reason. I need a bit of cheering up after my visit to Herbert Wilson with Communion this morning. The poor man is dying, and his body has been eaten away by cancer. There is nothing left of him. My wife prescribed a visit to you as the tonic I need.'

When I finished my confession, he raised his glass of stout and said, 'Here's to your dear lady. All I can say is that I'm flattered. Drink up, Vicar, and then we'll have one more before you go. Well, I can tell you that as far as the stage is concerned, everything is in order. There's only the opening and closing of the curtains to see to, and that's easy. What's not so easy is for you to get poor old

Herbert out of your mind. I don't know him very well. He never used to come to church. His wife was regular at Bethesda. He came here once to try to get me to do a life insurance. Typical Yorkshireman. He never really settled in Abergelly. That accent sticks out a mile.'

By the time I had consumed my second glass of stout, I had come to terms with myself. I shook hands with Tom on the doorstep. 'Thank you for your hospitality. My wife's prescription was the right one, as usual.'

'Well, as they do say, Vicar,' he replied, 'the show must go on.'

2

'The show must go on.' Tom Beynon's words echoed round my brain, as I looked at my watch. It was a quarter past seven and there was no sign of the Major-General and his daughter Kate. How could the show go on in the absence of one of the leading characters in the opera? There was no understudy available. The audience had already occupied more than half the seats in the Welfare Hall.

'I told you that you should not have allowed your Curate to risk a journey to Cardiff on the first night. You know what he is like.'

My wife's words had the effect of adding petrol to the fire of anger which was blazing inside me. 'For God's sake, woman, shut up!' I exploded.

She stared at me as if I were a stranger. I turned on my heels and stalked out towards the stage door. As I did so, Hugh Thomas and his fiancée erupted into the corridor, red-faced and breathless.

'Get in that dressing room!' I bellowed. 'I'll speak to you later. As for you, Janet, you had better get your skates on, you will be due on shortly.' As she ran to get into her costume and to be made up for the performance, tears trickled down her cheeks.

'There was no need for that,' remonstrated Hugh Thomas. 'It was not her fault.'

'I know whose fault it was,' I hissed. 'Now, hop it before I say something I may regret later.'

He disappeared in a five-yard dash he could never have equalled in his rugby career. I took a deep breath and made my way to the stage where the pirates had begun to take up their positions for the opening chorus. Outside, the orchestra was tuning up and a noisy audience was drowning the musical preparations.

'Have they turned up?' asked Bryn Matthews, empty flagon in hand.

'Yes,' I replied.

'It's OK, boys,' he shouted. 'They're here.' The chorus responded with a cheer.

'Do that when the curtain comes up,' I told them, 'and it will be brilliant.'

It was obvious that the relief they felt was going to be a vital factor in the quality of their performance. As far as I was concerned, my resentment was still smouldering. I found it difficult to settle down to my role as apprentice pirate after my altercation with the apprentice priest. Added to that was the realization that I had sworn at my wife. That was something I had never done before.

By the time the orchestra launched into the overture, I had seated myself on a 'rock' at the back of the stage with Ruth, the Pirate Maid of all Work, kneeling at my feet.

'Good luck!' whispered Elizabeth Williams.

'The same to you,' I replied, with a total lack of conviction. I was supposed to be in a despondent attitude when the curtains opened. I had never felt so despondent in my life. I began to wonder if I would remember my lines.

In the meanwhile, the pirates were excelling themselves with heart and lung in the opening chorus. Even Bryn Matthews appeared animated and his 'dance' included more hops than he had ever attempted in rehearsal. When Gareth Morgan entered as the Pirate King and slapped me violently on the shoulder, I was shaken out of my unhealthy introspection. It was the equivalent of a douche of cold water.

All went well until the entry of the chorus of girls, which was to be followed by the appearance of my wife as Mabel. I had to hold her hand 'very tenderly'. All through the chorus I wondered if I was to be confronted with a handful of rigid digits and a frozen smile. I was wrong. When she sang, 'Take heart, fair days will shine. Take any heart – take mine!' it was obvious that I was forgiven. We went off together and I kissed her when we reached the privacy of the wings.

'I must apologize profoundly for my outburst,' I said.

She put her fingers on my lips. 'Forget it, love,' she said. 'Let's concentrate on making this a really good first night.'

Before I could kiss her again Tom Beynon loomed up behind us. 'It's going great,' announced the stage manager. 'Nearly all seats taken, by the way. It'll be a sell-out for the rest of the week, believe me.'

By now, there was an influx of pirates, waiting excitedly to move on stage and catch hold of the young ladies. This was the highlight of the opera for the hot-blooded miners. They had needed no encouragement in rehearsals to indulge in realism. 'Don't overdo it, boys,' was my constant refrain in this part of the proceedings. As they crept on stage to ambush the Major-General's daughters, Eleanor turned to me in panic.

'Where's Hugh?' she whispered.

My Curate was due to appear any second on the platform centre stage to make a grand entrance. There was no time to speculate on his absence. Mabel and Frederic had to enter left, desperately hoping that the Major-General would arrive on time.

Samuel sang, 'We'd better pause or danger may befall, their father is a Major-General.'

'Yes, yes,' the girls repeated, 'he is a Major-General!'

The orchestra stopped and there was a silence which lasted an eternity. Eleanor grasped my hand. Suddenly there landed on the platform with an athletic leap an extremely youthful Major-General, the top of his tunic unbuttoned and his plumed hat at a rakish angle.

'Yes, I am a Major-General,' he proclaimed.

It must have been a source of great wonder to the audience how such a young man, who was minus his moustache, could have been father to so many young maidens. In a trice he was strutting across the stage, singing at a great pace the difficult patter song 'I am the very model of a modern Major-General'. Not a word was forgotten. The enunciation was impeccable. He dominated the scene and received an ovation. Obviously, the adrenaline was pumping into my Curate. His exchanges with the Pirate King produced a series of laughs. As the curtains came down on the finale of Act 1 to great applause, there was no doubt that the Abergelly Church Gilbert and Sullivan Society had made its mark in the town.

The first person to come up to me on the stage was Hugh Thomas.

'I'm sorry I've caused such trouble, Vicar,' he said, 'and I'm sorry I came on minus my moustache and with my uniform in such a mess. I was all fingers and thumbs. *Festina lente* was the school motto – 'Hasten slowly'. It is only now that the truth of that Latin tag has come home to me. I'll give you a graphic account of my travels after Matins tomorrow.'

'All is forgiven, Hugh,' I replied. 'But don't do it again, there's a good lad, otherwise I shall be developing stomach ulcers or heart attacks.'

'Shall I get Simeon Jones to put the moustache on me in the interval?' he asked.

'As it was in the beginning, is now and shall be until the end of the performance,' I replied. 'If you come on whiskered in Act 2 the audience will think you are doing a Jekyll and Hyde. Tomorrow night and for the rest of the week you will be seen as you should have been seen this evening.'

'Message received, chief,' he said, and made his way to his beloved, who was waiting for him in the wings.

'Oh, dry the glistening tear' was the opening chorus of Act 2. Janet's glistening tears had given way to a look of undeserved adoration as her beloved came to meet her, fresh from his triumph in Act 1.

Inevitably the funniest moment in Act 2 was provided by Willie James in the entry of the policemen. He dropped his truncheon accidentally, and tried to recover it as they made a second circuit of the stage, falling down in the process of making a quick snatch at the baton. He had the effrontery to make an elaborate bow of appreciation to the audience as they howled their laughter. At the curtain call, as each principal came forward to receive their portion of the applause, Willie proceeded to wave his truncheon to draw attention to himself. No sooner had Tom Beynon pulled the drapes across than all the policemen dived upon him and eventually raised him from the floor, a dishevelled figure who looked very sorry for himself.

'What did the Vicar say about teamwork?' grumbled Ivor Hodges.

'Calm down, everybody,' I shouted. 'Well done, keep this up for the rest of the week and our society will be the talk of the town.'

No sooner had I finished speaking than Graham Webb came through the curtains. He played a different tune.

'Girls, your first entry was a musical mess. Keep your eye on me. You were competing with the orchestra and not working with them. Gentlemen, your joint chorus in Act 2 fell apart at the end. The tenors in the pirates group were shouting their top notes, not singing them. As far as the police were concerned, I know that the music calls for pianissimo. That does not mean inaudibility. Principals, after a nervous start you improved as time went on. What I said to the girls applies to you. Keep a wary eye on me and all will be well. Anyway, for a first night the singing was more than passable. One last thing – watch your diction.'

'You can tell he's a schoolteacher,' said Dai Elbow when Graham had gone from the stage to talk to the orchestra.

'Enough of that talk,' riposted Ivor Hodges. 'You are talking about a fellow member of my profession. Yes he is a schoolmaster, and a very good one at that. What's more, he's a very good musical director as well.' There was a chorus of hear, hears.

That night as Eleanor and I relaxed in our sitting room, sipping our tumblers of whisky, she said, 'That was quite an eventful evening. I wondered at the beginning whether we would have to cancel it. No wonder you were so over-wrought. Perhaps we should invest in understudies from now on.'

'That's easier said than done,' I replied. 'We are hardly blessed with a wealth of talent.'

'You never know,' went on my wife. 'After seeing how well the show has gone, we may get a batch of new recruits, including some from other societies in the valley. By the way, I wonder what disaster delayed Hugh and Janet. She was very distressed and didn't really recover her composure throughout the show.'

'Tomorrow morning,' I said, 'I shall hear the whole saga after Matins when my Curate has promised that he will reveal all. I hope it's a valid excuse.'

Hugh Thomas was in an exuberant mood when he entered the vestry. 'Good morning, Vicar. What a lovely day!' he enthused.

'I know it is not raining but it is a miserable grey morning,' I said. 'Perhaps you had not noticed that after your bravura performance last night. Well, let's get into the church and say our prayers.'

He provided a histrionic reading of the lessons. Since the first was a series of regulations from Leviticus and the second was a rather obscure chapter from the Epistle to the Hebrews, it was quite a feat. I think he would have read the bus timetable in Abergelly Square in similar fashion, given his obvious feeling of exultation. After the service was over, he said, 'Would you like to have my explanation about my near disaster now or later this morning?'

'I think you had better come to the Vicarage for a coffee now. That will leave you free to do some visiting in Brynfelin this morning and in the early afternoon,' I replied.

'Vicar, you are a slave-driver,' was his amused comment.

Eleanor was leaving for her surgery as we came down the drive. 'I hope you will be earlier at the Welfare Hall tonight,' she said. 'It will be nice to see you with your grey moustache, your collar buttoned up and your headgear at a dignified angle. Your entry last night was more like that of Errol Flynn than of an aged general.'

'Dr Secombe,' he replied, 'I promise you that I shall be first in the chair to receive our make-up artist's attentions. The Vicar will supply you with the reasons for my unfortunate absence once I have unburdened myself.'

'Hugh, you are incorrigible,' she said.

As we sat in my study drinking Mrs Cooper's instant coffee, my Curate unburdened himself. 'Everything went well after we set out for Cardiff. We had an easy run into the city. Not much traffic on the roads and no parking problems. When we got there, Janet did some shopping while I spent a happy hour or so browsing in the book-shops. We had arranged to meet outside the City Hall at one o'clock. At a quarter to one I left WH Smith's to go to the appointed meeting place. Outside the bookshop I bumped into Dewi Williams. I hadn't seen him since we were in college together. He is a Curate in one of the

Cardiff parishes. By the time we had finished chatting, I realized it was a quarter past one. I made an undignified dash up Queen Street, with my clerical collar half undone. When I got to the City Hall, there was no sign of Janet. I waited ten minutes or so and then decided to go to the car park where I had left my jalopy in case she had thought I might be there. I arrived only to find no sign of her. I stayed for about a quarter of an hour, to no avail. The only alternative was to go back to the City Hall. By now I was beginning to wonder when this game of hide and seek would end.'

'So am I!' I interjected. 'Don't tell me that you spent the next two or three hours chasing each other around Cardiff.'

'Sorry, Vicar,' he said. 'Well, to cut a long story short, when I got back she was standing outside the City Hall looking very woebegone.'

'I don't doubt that!' I said.

'Well, we had a snack in a café in Queen Street,' he went on. 'It was three o'clock when we got back to the car, plenty of time to reach Abergelly for the show. The blessed car wouldn't start. There was plenty of petrol in the tank. The battery was OK, I thought. After several attempts to get the thing going; the battery gave up the ghost. I put the bonnet up and fiddled around with the wires. To be honest, Vicar, I am no mechanic. There was only thing – to ring the RAC. It took them half an hour to arrive. Apparently there was something wrong with the solenoid. By the time he had gone somewhere to find a replacement for my vintage mechanism and then recharged the battery, it was gone five o'clock. When we got out of the car park we got caught in the rush hour traffic coming out of Cardiff. Never again, Vicar, I promise you. As I said to Dr Secombe, I shall be first in Simeon's chair tonight, believe me.'

'I believe you,' I replied. 'I hope this has taught you a lesson to get your priorities right. The trip to Cardiff could have waited until next week.'

For the rest of the week *The Pirates of Penzance* sailed in calmer waters. The chorus and the principals gathered confidence as the nights went by. Graham Webb and his orchestra were at peace with each other by the last performance. The local press had delivered a favourable review with a headline 'Successful Launch in Abergelly'. On the Saturday night we held a party on the stage to celebrate the birth of the society. The chorus men had clubbed together to buy a small barrel of beer and the females brought home-made Welsh cakes and sandwiches to complement the drink.

'It's a change to have a full tankard instead of an empty one,' said Bryn Matthews.

'Where 'ave you been?' asked Dai Elbow. 'I've 'ad plenty of liquid in mine every night. 'Ow can you sing "Pour, oh pour the pirate sherry" with nothing to drink? I've gone through three bottles of rhubarb wine since Monday.'

'No wonder you were drowning the rest of us tonight,' commented Willie James.

'You'd better shut up,' riposted Dai. 'Who's the one that 'as been shouting louder than everybody else in the pirate scenes and then trying to do a Charlie Chaplin act as a policeman – and that was without a drop of 'ow's your father. It would have been God 'elp us if you'd 'ad some liquor inside you.'

'Quite right,' said Ivor Hodges. 'As your sergeant I would have had you for larceny. A bad case of scene-stealing every night. I thought you would have stopped that after the boys gave you a going over on Monday. But your ego is so big in your little body that even a steam-roller could not squash it.'

'Gentlemen!' I shouted. 'Let's have order, as they say in the Workingmen's Club. First, let me say a big thank you to everybody for a job well done. It is not easy to embark on a venture like this when almost all of you are strangers to this form of stagework. I think I can safely say that you have enjoyed it (hear, hear) and that you are ready for a second helping next year (louder agreement). We shall have a break and then get to work again next September with a produc-tion of *The Mikado*.' (Cries of 'ooh' from the girls.)

There was no 'ooh' from my wife. She came across to me in high dudgeon. 'Since when was that decided, Frederick?' she demanded. 'I thought that for our next epic I was supposed to be in charge of production and you were to be the comic lead. That was too much to expect. You just love being Pooh-Bah. If you could, you would play Pooh-Bah and Koko at the same time, as well as being director.' This conversation was conducted out of sight of the cast in the prompt corner of the stage, to which I had been led almost forcibly by my spouse.

'Now, calm down, love,' I said, as her tirade finished. 'I apologize for my indiscretion and my sins are ever before me. I am afraid I got carried away and wished to end my few words on a high note.'

'Another few words like that and you will be carried away on a stretcher,' she replied through clenched teeth, 'ending with an even higher note.'

'My dear girl,' I began.

'Don't "dear girl" me,' she breathed. 'The last thing I want to hear from you is condescension. You may be Vicar of the parish, I accept that, but you are not Vicar of this society. From now on, this is truly a joint venture. Between us we shall decide what show we are going to put on, and if it means something other than *Mikado*, so be it. Now then, I think we had better go back and join the party, otherwise they may think that something is amiss.'

She stormed off with her glass of white wine, leaving me standing in a daze. I decided to put a smile on my face, consoled by the knowledge that next year's 'few words' would have to be spoken by Eleanor.

Next morning Tom Beynon came into the vestry after the eight o' clock Communion service, his face beaming. 'Great show last night, Vicar. What's more, ten communicants up on last Sunday. Lots of compliments when they were going out. Say what you like, a lively parish will bring more people to church, even if it takes *The Pirates of Penzance* to do it. By the way, I shall be at the Welfare Hall this morning to take down the scenery. Ivor Hodges will be in charge here, even if he wakes up with a hangover.'

When I went back to the Vicarage, Mrs Cooper had prepared an excellent breakfast of bacon and eggs. All my time in my previous parish I had fasted until lunchtime. Eleanor informed me, in her medical capacity, that in the interests of my digestive condition it would be wise to have something inside my stomach once I had fasted for my early morning Communion. As I sat at the table, enjoying the repast in the company of my wife and family, I felt I had to apologize for my gaffe of the previous evening. The matrimonial bed had been a back-to-back exercise.

'Thank you, Mrs Cooper,' I said. 'This is delicious, isn't it, children?'

'Yummy, yummy,' said Elspeth with her mouth full.

'Bang on,' added David when our housekeeper-cum-nanny had gone out of the room. I touched Eleanor's knee under the table. She looked up from her plate and turned her attention to me.

'Sorry about the *Mikado* episode,' I said quietly. 'It was quite unwarranted. You choose whatever you want to do next.'

'This is not the place, nor the time, to discuss that,' she replied in mock censorial tones. Then she smiled as she went on, 'How about a little chat on the subject this evening after church in the sitting room, and perhaps in the bedroom?' She caressed my knee under the table. I went to the Family Communion service in good heart.

To my surprise, when I mounted the pulpit steps to deliver my homily I discovered that there was a row of the Major-General's daughters in one of the back pews of the church. A warm glow at the sight of the girls made itself felt as I embarked upon the Gospel for the day, part of the Sermon on the Mount: 'Do not be anxious about tomorrow. Tomorrow will look after itself. Each day has troubles enough of its own.'

I decided to begin with an off-the-cuff illustration prompted by the appearance of the girls and other members of the cast, among them some of the principals, including the Sergeant of Police, Ruth the Maid of all Work and the Pirate King, who should have been at the daughter church. 'When last Monday arrived with no sign of the costumes for our performance at the Welfare Hall, I must admit that I was very worried about the morrow. Then on Tuesday I was even more worried about the absence of one of the principals with just a quarter of an hour to go before the curtain up. I should have realized that the very existence of the Society was an act of faith. Twelve months ago the baby had not even been born. Now it is in good health with a splendid future ahead. It is this kind of faith which must imbue our individual lives.'

By the time I had finished, ten minutes later, I had become convinced that I had done the right thing in founding the Society. The girls had listened attentively to my words. Were it not for their membership of Abergelly G and S, they would not have been in church that morning.

After service when I came from the vestry I found that Eleanor and the children were engaged in conversation with them.

'They want to know if they can join the choir,' said my wife.

'By all means,' I replied. 'We shall have to get robes for you. There is plenty of room for you in the choir stalls. Friday night at half past seven is choir practice, if you turn up there, but perhaps by that time we might have been able to get the robes and then find you have not turned up.'

There was a chorus of response that it was a firm commitment.

'Can I join the choir?' asked Elspeth. The girls laughed.

'Why are they laughing, Daddy?' she went on.

'It's because you will have to grow up a lot more before you can be a chorister,' I said. 'You are only four now. When you are fourteen, then you will be able to be with the girls.'

When we were relaxing after our Sunday lunch, Eleanor said, 'Well, the evangelistic outreach of your histrionic activity was well to the fore this morning. Not only have you found some good voices for your choir but you have some confirmation fodder, I would say.'

'Confirmation fodder!' I exclaimed. 'You could have put that more delicately as "possible confirmation candidates".'

'Let me tell you something else, Vicar,' she added. 'Your confirmation candidates have persuaded the female producer of your next show that it will have to be *The Mikado*. They were so enthusiastic about being Japanese schoolchildren that I could not have dampened their ardour by saying, "We must wait and see." So there, Reverend Pooh-Bah.'

'My dear love, you can't have a diminutive Pooh-Bah. It will have to be Gareth Morgan with his second-row forward physique. Anyway, I am so glad you have decided to do *The Mikado*. It's always a crowd-puller. By the way, I wonder why Gareth was down here instead of being at his own church. Perhaps it was some inkling he had that other members of the cast were coming after last week's success. I noticed that his wife wasn't with him.'

'I noticed, too,' said Eleanor, 'that he spent some time after church talking to Janice Walters. You will have to keep a wary eye open for an illicit affair. Janice is only seventeen.' She was a vivacious redhead in the sixth form of Ivor Hodges' school.

'I think you are barking up the wrong tree there,' I replied. 'Gareth is not that kind of bloke, and in any case he is devoted to his dearly beloved.'

'You can never be too sure,' said my wife. 'Operatic societies are noted for that sort of thing.'

The following day, after Matins, Hugh Thomas came to the Vicarage for coffee. His morale was high. The adrenaline of the previous week was still coursing through his being.

'I think we have made quite an impact on the town,' he announced in ringing tones.

'The next impact we have to make, Hugh,' I replied, 'will require much more than a week. We must put *The Pirates of Penzance* behind us and concentrate on the spiritual needs of the parish as well as the necessity of raising the money to build a permanent church at Brynfelin. In a fortnight's time we shall be holding the talent service. That will provide the thermometer of the amount of dedication in the congregation.'

Six months previously members of the congregation had each been given one pound to multiply and bring back to the altar. Now the moment of truth was near at hand. Dai Elbow had used his pound to bet on his greyhound and had already raised more than forty pounds. He had told me on Saturday night that he hoped to reach three figures 'by D-Day', as he put it. On a much smaller scale, other parishioners had been producing home-made cakes, home-made dolls and even patchwork quilts. There was a sense of excitement in the air as the time for the presentation of the multiplied pounds grew closer.

'If it is anything to go by,' said my Curate, 'from what I can gather, that thermometer will be near the top. Take my landlady, for example: she seems to spend all her spare time knitting tea cosies and that sort of thing. Apparently they are selling like mad.'

'Let's hope you are right, Hugh,' I replied. 'However, that leaves what I first mentioned, the spiritual needs of the parish which have to be addressed. The number of confirmations has not been high over the past ten years. We must have a drive to raise the number considerably before classes begin next month. You will be pleased to know that six of your daughters turned up at church yesterday morning and have asked to join the choir. I should think that they would be candidates for confirmation. Not only were they present, but Gareth Morgan turned up as well when he should have been with you at Brynfelin.'

'I have been meaning to talk to you about Gareth,' said my curate, looking somewhat embarrassed. 'He seems to be taking a –' he paused, '– more than an acceptable interest in Janice Walters. She is flattered because he is a good-looking older man. It is a pity his wife didn't stay with the society. As you know, when she saw how young the girls in the chorus were, she stopped coming. I suppose I should have told you earlier. Still, it is a good thing that Janice is joining the parish church choir. That will keep them apart for the time being.'

'I must tell you, Hugh,' I replied, 'my wife told me that she saw him talking to Janice after church and warned me to keep an eye on things. I said that Gareth was not that kind of man. It looks as if I was wrong.'

3

'Come on in, Vicar. How nice to see you.' Marion Morgan greeted me with a warm smile when I knocked at the door of 13 Glamorgan Terrace at Brynfelin. She was an attractive brunette in her late twenties. 'I'm sorry Gareth is not in. He is helping Hugh Thomas at the youth club.'

I had decided to pay an early evening visit to the Morgan residence after my Curate's disturbing information that morning. The sooner the relationship with Janice Walters was nipped in the bud the better, I felt.

'Is there anything you want to see him about?' she said.

'It's just a social call,' I said, with a twinge of conscience at the little white lie. 'Please sit down,' she invited. 'Can I offer you a drink? A whisky or a sherry?'

'A whisky with a fair amount of water would be fine, thank you,' I replied.

'I'll bring a jug of water and you can pour it in yourself in case I drown it.'

So saying she disappeared, while I sat in the leather armchair surveying the front room, or parlour as the town council described it. On the mantelpiece was a wedding photograph of a very happy couple, flanked by portraits of bride and groom in their late teens. The earlier twinge of conscience now became a pang as I realized that if I had not created the Abergelly Gilbert and Sullivan Society this domestic bliss would have been unimpaired. So much for my evangelistic outreach. When Marion returned with my drink she was full of enthusiasm for the society's performance of *The Pirates of Penzance*.

'I only saw the opening night and the last night, I am trying to finish some pencil sketches of St Peter's which have been ordered for the talent scheme. Everybody was wonderful, even Gareth! I never thought he could act – sing, yes, but act, no. He really surprised me. I would have loved to have been part of it. I could never have fitted in with all those young girls.'

'When we start again in September, Marion,' I said, 'You must come to the rehearsals and make the tea for the interval. In fact, I think you look young enough to be in the chorus. My wife is going to be in charge of the production of *The Mikado*. I am sure she would be pleased to have you. In any case, don't be out of it, whether it is making tea or singing in the chorus.'

'That's very kind of you, Vicar,' she replied. 'I'll take you up on that.'

When I left the house I went to the prefab tabernacle to look in on Hugh Thomas's youth club. As I got out of my car I could hear rock and roll music disturbing the peace of Brynfelin. The noise, as I opened the door, was deafening. A dozen or so young girls were gyrating in what was the nave of the church watched by an even bigger number of youths, while four lads were playing table tennis in what was left of the space near the altar rails. Hugh and Janet were engaged in earnest conversation by the large amplifier which was supplying the music. There was no sign of Gareth. I threaded my way through the throng to the couple, who were oblivious to the torrent of decibels emanating from the infernal machine. I tapped Hugh on the shoulder. He shot up in the air and then turned around to discover his Vicar standing alongside him.

'Could you possibly reduce the level of sound?' I shouted.

He moved across to the turntable of the radiogram which stood alongside the altar and twiddled with the knobs. As Bill Haley and his Comets receded suddenly into a more moderate volume of performance, the dancers and the watchers switched their attention to the sanctuary in obvious annoyance at the interference with their pleasure.

'Carry on dancing,' called my Curate.

'Is it always as loud as this?' I asked him.

'That's the way they like it.'

'Is that the way the neighbours like it?' I replied. 'Surely you must have had complaints about the noise?'

'None at all,' said Hugh, and Janet, anxious to support her fiancée, added the information that though her house was not far away, none of her neighbours had ever said anything about it.

'In that case, you can increase the volume once I have gone,' I replied. 'Where is Gareth?'

My Curate looked puzzled. 'I haven't the faintest idea, Vicar. Why do you ask?' 'According to his wife, he is supposed to be helping you.'

'Not to my knowledge. He called in once not long after I opened the club. That is the only occasion he has been here.' Hugh looked at me. 'Trouble, isn't it?'

'Big trouble,' I replied. 'We must have a talk about this after Matins tomorrow. If something is not done soon, a happy marriage could be wrecked, and a young girl's career with it.'

As I went out through the door Bill Haley's music bade me an ear-shattering farewell. It was a great relief to get into the quiet of my car and make my way back to the Vicarage.

Before I could get out of my Ford 8, there was a tap on the window. I opened the car door.

'Don't get out!' ordered Eleanor. 'Evan Roberts has had a heart attack. They have taken him to the hospital but it looks as if it is a vain hope. Will you go to Ward 3? Eirwen is in a terrible state. I could hardly make out what she was saying over the phone.'

Evan Roberts was the parish church organist and Eirwen, his wife, was one of the few troublemakers in the parish. I reversed the car and raced up the drive in a shower of gravel. At the hospital, I abandoned the car rather than parked it and ran to the entrance. The receptionist looked up from her perusal of a list.

'Ward 3, Vicar,' she said, 'but I am afraid you are too late.'

Forearmed with this information, I prepared myself to cope with Eirwen Roberts. The ward door was open and I went into the sister's office, where she was engaged in conversation with the consultant. They stopped their talk and turned their attention on me.

'I'm afraid Mr Roberts has died some ten minutes ago. Mrs Roberts will be glad of any comfort you can give her. She is in the waiting room with her daughter.' The sister stood up. 'I'll come with you.'

Mr Aneurin Williams, the consultant, then addressed me. 'It was a massive heart attack, Vicar. Considering the state of his heart, it is a wonder that this did not happen some time ago.'

As I went down the corridor with Sister Llewellyn, my mind's eye conjured up the vision which would confront me. It was accurate in every detail. A loud wail greeted me when I entered the room. The widow was seated in a chair, with her daughter's arms around her. I went across to her and sat in the chair beside her. She jerked herself up.

'Why has God done this, Vicar? Evan was a good man, never did any harm to anybody. He was looking forward to being retired next year. Now, he's gone in a flash. It's not fair. We could have had some lovely years together. We'd made plans to go on holidays and things like that.'

The longer the monologue went on, the more convinced I became that the Lord had decided happiness should come to poor Evan now and not tomorrow. I tried to hold her hand. It was like trying to hold that of a recalcitrant child. She rejected my attention.

'Other men can go drinking and carry on with women and things like that and nothing happens to them. You take old Arthur Evans up the road. He's led a terrible life and there he is as fit as a fiddle, and he's eighty. Evan was only sixty-four last August.' She paused in her tirade only to indulge in another wail.

'I'll leave you with her, Vicar,' said the sister and left the room quickly.

Evelyn Hopkins, the widow's daughter, made a vain attempt to subdue the noisy grief. 'Come on, bear up, love. Let the Vicar say some prayers. That will help, I'm sure.'

I stood up to address the Almighty.

'Prayers won't bring him back,' shouted Eirwen.

'I am going to pray for the repose of his soul, Mrs Roberts,' I said firmly, 'and to pray that God will give you strength to face the days ahead.'

'Go ahead, then,' she bellowed. 'Much good that will do.'

I ignored the remark and launched into extempore prayer, trying desperately to concentrate my mind against the competition of the continued wailing. Suddenly it stopped. Shortage of breath, I thought. I was wrong. The rest of my prayer was heard in silence.

'Shall we say together the Lord's Prayer?' I said, after the end of my somewhat rambling supplication. There was a long silence afterwards. I sat down beside the widow, whose breath was coming in gulps. This time she allowed me to hold her hand.

'I'm sorry, Vicar,' she murmured. 'It's been such a shock. He went out to work this morning as right as rain. Had a good dinner when he came home, sat in his chair, reading the *Western Mail* as he always did. I went into the kitchen to do the washing up. I hadn't been in there five minutes when I heard a noise.' She stopped and began to shed tears quietly. 'I found him spread out on the floor face down. I turned him over. His eyes were closed. I thought for a moment he was dead but when I felt his pulse I could see that he was still alive. I ran out of the house to Maggie Williams up at number seven. She's the only one in the street with a phone. Fair play, the ambulance was there in no time, but it was no use. He was only in hospital for about an hour and then he was gone.'

The wailing began again. To my great relief the sister returned. 'Would you like to come and see your husband, Mrs Roberts? Do you want to see him on your own or do you want your daughter and the Vicar to come with you?'

The widow dabbed her eyes with her handkerchief. 'I can't face that on my own,' she replied. 'I'll be needing all the help I can get now.'

'You'll get that, Mam,' said her daughter. 'Won't she, Vicar?'

'Of course,' I replied, 'everybody at St Peter's will want to do what they can to help you in your time of trouble.'

For a moment, the widow forgot her grief. 'All I can say to that, Vicar, is that I hope they will do more for me than they did for Annie Perkins in her time of trouble.' Annie Perkins was the widow of the obnoxious churchwarden I had inherited from my predecessor when I came to Abergelly. I chose to ignore the remark and left the waiting room with the others to view the faithful departed.

Eleanor wanted a full account of the evening's proceedings when I came home.

'Lucky Evan,' she said when I had finished my description of the events at the hospital. 'Now poor Evelyn will be the recipient of Eirwen's attentions, and of course the congregation at St Peter's. The next thing is, who will take Evan's place at the organ?'

'I was thinking about that on my way home,' I replied. 'The obvious choice is Graham Webb. I don't know whether he can play the organ or not. If he can't he can keep his feet off the pedals until he learns how to use them. In any case, Evan more often than not had his feet on the wrong ones, as you well know. I'll give him a ring tomorrow, or better still, call in at the school during the lunch break. I can let Ivor know about Evan's death at the same time. By the way, I paid a visit to 13 Glamorgan Terrace only to find Marion Morgan on her own. She had been busy doing some pencil sketches of St Peter's to sell for the talent scheme. She said that Gareth had gone down to help Hugh Thomas at the youth club. When I arrived at St David's Hugh informed me that Gareth never came there except for one brief visit just after the club opened.'

'What a stupid man!' exploded Eleanor. 'With a pretty young wife like Marion, why has he got to go messing about with a schoolgirl? You will have to do something about it at once, before something serious develops.'

'I have told Marion that she must come to rehearsals when we start again,' I replied. 'I said that perhaps she could join the chorus since she is only in her late twenties or, if not, help with the tea for the interval.'

'Of course she can come into the chorus, she is a young-looking lady in any case, but that does not solve the problem of Gareth's philandering. The next rehearsals are months away. Now is the time to act,' retorted my wife.

'Hugh and I are going to discuss the matter after Matins tomorrow,' I said.

She exploded once again. 'It doesn't call for discussion, Fred. It is your responsibility to approach that man and lay down the law. The Curate doesn't come into it. You are the Vicar, and you will have to get that man on his own some time this weekend. Maybe you can put an end to it without Marion knowing what has happened. It would break her heart if she was told that her beloved

Gareth was carrying on with a schoolgirl. You talk to Hugh about it tomorrow by all means, but you are the person who must take some action. The buck stops with you, as Truman put it.'

The next morning my worried-looking Curate followed me into my study after Matins. 'What are we going to do, Vicar?' he asked.

'Sit down, Hugh,' I said. 'It is not a question of what are we going to do. I have decided that this is my problem. One day this week I am going to get Gareth down at the Vicarage by some means or other and I shall lay down the law.'

'Couldn't I leave a written note from you when I go visiting at Brynfelin tomorrow?' suggested my Curate. 'You can say that you want to see him urgently.' 'I'll be glad of your help in pushing the note through his letterbox tomorrow afternoon,' I replied, 'but I think you must leave the wording to me. If I use the word "urgently" he may smell a rat or come with a plausible tale to cover his tracks. I must catch him completely by surprise. I shall think over what I shall say and you can pick up the note tomorrow when you come for our morning prayers.'

At 12.30 p.m. I entered the Abergelly Secondary Modern School in search of Graham Webb. I had to thread my way through a horde of chattering schoolchildren to get to the staffroom, where several teachers were in the process of unwrapping their packed lunches. One of them was Graham. He looked up in surprise when he saw me.

'Don't say we are starting rehearsals next week,' he said.

'Nothing of the sort,' I replied. 'Can you play an organ?'

He eyed me with even greater surprise. 'Yes, I can, but not very expertly, I'm afraid. I am a pianist, not an organist.'

'Would you mind coming back to my car with me for a few minutes?' I asked. 'I am sorry to delay your lunch but it will only be for a few minutes, I can assure you.'

I had parked my car outside the school gates, away from the prying eyes of the pupils. As we sat in the front seats, he said, 'Well, Vicar, please explain your cloak and dagger behaviour.'

'To put it bluntly,' I replied, 'our organist died suddenly last night and we need a new man to replace him.'

'You certainly don't let the grass grow under your feet!' he remarked. 'All I can say is that I will help you out for the moment. I don't know whether I can commit myself to a permanent arrangement. The weekend is an oasis for me in a busy life. As you know, I live with my widowed mother and she relies on me to be the handyman and the gardener. What is more, it is the only time I have to do some reading. Could you give me some idea of what is involved in being your organist?'

'First of all, Graham, thank you for helping out for the time being,' I said. 'You would have to be at the 9.30 a.m. Family Communion and the 6.30 p.m. Evensong. Choir practice is on Friday evenings at 7.30 p.m. Then, of course, there are the weddings. We have, on average, about forty to fifty in the year.'

He whistled quietly. 'So that means my Saturdays will be swallowed up as well as my Sundays. That is quite a big undertaking. You must give me some time to think this over. In the meantime, I shall come down for choir practice on Friday.'

'Would you like to come to dinner beforehand?' I asked. 'I could let you know about the hymns, for example. I pick them for the month and the organist chooses the tunes. The psalms are set in the lectionary. We could have the meal early and that would give you a chance to look at the organ.'

'That's a deal,' he replied. 'I shall come straight from school. Now, I must get back to my lunch, if you don't mind.'

'I'm very grateful to you, Graham,' I said. 'Would you apologize to Ivor Hodges for my intrusion into his staffroom without his permission? You can tell him that it was for a good cause. He will be shocked to learn that Evan Roberts has died. I was going to see him, but on second thoughts, I'll call round to see him tonight. Like you, he will be anxious to have his lunch.'

My lunch was waiting for me when I arrived at the Vicarage. Mrs Cooper had prepared sausage and laver bread, one of my favourite meals.

'This is seaweed, isn't it, Dad?' said David. 'Elspeth wouldn't believe me.'

'Yes, it is seaweed, but it is a special kind of seaweed, Elspeth. Not the kind you see when you go down to the bays.'

'Ugh!' my daughter pushed her plate away. 'That'th horrid,' she lisped. 'It lookth horrid too.'

'Don't be silly,' said my wife. 'You eat that up. It's very good for you. You want to grow up to be a nice healthy girl, don't you?'

Elspeth nodded her head violently.

'Then eat it up while it's hot. Mummy has brought it all the way from Cardiff especially for you.'

Very gingerly she pulled the plate towards her and tentatively poked her fork into the black substance. 'Can I give it to Lulu?' she asked. Lulu was our Crufts-registered bitch who had an affair with an Alsatian and put paid to our hopes for some lucrative breeding.

'Of course not!' snapped Eleanor. 'Lulu has dog food. She wouldn't like laver bread, anyway. Now are you going to eat it up or not?'

Our daughter decided not to risk any further disobedience and put a modicum in her mouth. Finding that she liked it, she proceeded to clear her plate, pointing out that David had left some of his.

'David'th naughty, isn't he?' she said, only too glad to have her own back on her brother for starting the 'seaweed' episode.

'No, I'm not!' he retorted. 'It's rude to clear your plate, isn't it, Mum?'

'Of course it's not,' said Eleanor. 'Who told you that?'

'Nana Davies,' he replied. My mother-in-law was an unmitigated snob.

'Well, she's wrong,' said my wife firmly. 'She is not a doctor like your grandfather was. I am sure he would have told you to eat up all your food.'

Elspeth preened herself.

'Come on, children, let's get ready now,' announced Mrs Cooper, 'otherwise you are going to be late. I'll see to the dishes, Dr Secombe, when I come back.'

There was the usual dash for the lavatory which David always won. Five minutes later Eleanor and I were on our own.

'Well,' said my wife, 'what is the result of your meeting with Graham?'

'It was most productive,' I replied. 'He will be here for a meal before choir practice next Friday. He says that he will take on the post for the time being, but he will not commit himself to a permanent undertaking until he has thought it over. His free weekend is not something he will sacrifice easily. Still, I feel he will take the job once he has got into the swing of things. I am much more worried about this Gareth Morgan business. What am I going to put into the note that will not make him suspicious?'

'Come off it, Frederick,' she said sharply. 'All it needs is something to the effect that you want to see him about matters up at St David's. It's just a little white lie. It is not even that. If he is going to persist with their relationship then he will have to pack in as churchwarden. So to that extent it does involve St David's, very much so. What is more important is how you are going to make it plain to him that the affair, if you can call it that, stops immediately, before a lot of hurt is caused. My dear love, you will have to be very firm. I know it is not in your character to be confrontational but this is one occasion when you will have to be.'

Ten minutes later we parted, she to do her home visits and I to make my way to the church hall to address the Mothers' Union, a group of women who had long ceased to be childbearing. The president was a seventy-year-old spinster, a Vicar's daughter. Miss Emily Aitken was a tall, painfully thin lady whose shoulders were permanently bent. Her sparse grey hair was gathered into a bun which bristled with hairpins. A pince-nez was perched on her beaky nose. She was a formidable figure. When I entered the hall there was a babble of conversation among the twenty or so members. Winnie Beynon, the church-warden's wife, was giving out the Mothers' Union prayer books. Agnes Jones was practising 'Hark my soul, it is the Lord' on the piano. It was a tentative performance. Miss Aitken was thumbing through the pages of a Bible. When she saw me she came to greet me with her bony hand out-stretched.

'Oh, Vicar,' she said in parsonical tones, obviously inherited from her father. 'Please take a seat.' She pointed to a chair behind the table where she had been examining the holy scriptures.

'How nice to see you,' she went on. 'We shall be start-ing our service in a few minutes.' Then raising her thin reedy voice, she enquired, 'Who are doing the tea for this afternoon?' Two ladies in the back row of chairs put up their hands, as if they were pupils in a classroom.

'It's all ready in the kitchen, Miss Aitken,' said Bronwen Pugh, who was a member of the Parochial Church Council and one of the biggest gossips in the congregation.

I took my seat alongside the president. Having found the elusive passage in the Bible, she stood up and addressed the group.

'First of all, let me say how good it is to have our Vicar with us this afternoon. I am sure we are all looking for-ward to what he has to say to us. Now then, I have a few announcements to make. Don't forget that next Sunday will be the big day when we come to present our multi-plied talents at the altar. I hear that some of you have done great things with our talents. Well done! The Vicar will be pleased to know that, won't you, Vicar?' I nodded. 'Next Wednesday, our speaker will be Miss Rosemary Thomas who will give us a talk on her visit to the Holy Land. She will be bringing slides with her. Now, last of all, I have to announce the death of Mr Evan Roberts, the husband of one of our most devoted members, Mrs Eirwen Roberts. I hope you will make an effort to attend the funeral service at St Peter's, whenever it is.'

Bronwen Pugh stood up at the back. 'I hear that they have made provisional arrangements for the funeral. Is that right, Vicar?'

'Not as yet, Mrs Pugh,' I replied from my chair.

'I shall begin our service with a reading from St John's Gospel, the fourteenth chapter, verses one to fourteen.' Miss Aitken intoned the first seven verses impeccably but ran into trouble with the eighth. 'Philip saith unto him, Lord show us the Father and it suffitheth uth –' she coughed delicately '– and it is sufficient for us,' she continued triumphantly, avoiding a further fiasco with 'sufficeth us'. She then proceeded to the prayers from the Mothers' Union handbook, including one for Evan Roberts, who had been granted provincial status by Bronwen Pugh, and one for his widow, 'our beloved sister'.

'Now then, shall we all join in the Mothers' Union prayer: "Help us to be faithful wives and loving mothers"?' intoned the septuagenarian spinster.

When the prayers ended, she announced that we would sing hymn number 24. 'Number 24,' she repeated in true clerical style. Agnes Jones thumped a discordant chord on the piano. Then began an unseemly race between the singers and Agnes, in which the pianist was playing the last few notes of each verse after the ladies had finished their contribution.

'There is no need for me to introduce our Vicar,' said Miss Aitken. 'I do not know what he is going to talk about, but I am sure it will be most interesting, as usual.'

For twenty minutes I delivered a rambling discourse on Christian family life. As the numbers of those whose eyelids began to droop increased, I brought my peroration to a sudden end.

'Shall we show our appreciation in the usual way?' announced the president. The applause was muted from my semi-somnolent audience, who had been startled by the abrupt conclusion. It resembled the greeting given to a tail-end batsman on his return to the pavilion on the Abergelly cricket ground. Bronwen Pugh and her helpers made their way to the kitchen to make the tea. Agnes Jones abandoned her place at the piano and announced that she was collecting the money for seats on the annual outing to Porthcawl. There was now a hubbub of conversation from the members as they awaited the arrival of the tea and biscuits.

'You will stay for a cup of tea, Vicar?' said Miss Aitken.

'If you don't mind,' I replied, 'I am afraid I shall have to slip away directly I have had my tea. I have a very busy schedule. You know what it is like.'

'I do indeed,' she commented. 'As a Vicar's daughter I know how hectic a parson's life can be. The ordinary lay person has no idea of what is entailed.'

At this juncture in the conversation, Bronwen Pugh arrived with a tray laden with two cups of tea and a plate of biscuits. 'I must say, Vicar, how much we all enjoyed

The Pirates of Penzance. I thought you and Dr Secombe were really lovely in your duets and things. As for the Curate, he was a scream, wasn't he?'

Before she could say any more, she was stopped in her tracks by her supremo. 'The Vicar has got to get away.'

Bronwen glared at her and retired to the kitchen in high dudgeon at the loss of five minutes' gossip with the Vicar.

I was halfway through my second Marie biscuit when the hall was invaded by a band of gypsies. All the talking ceased as the astonished Mothers' Union watched them come up to me at the table. They were led by a matriarch who acted as spokeswoman.

'Sorry to trouble you, Reverend, but the lady at your house said we would find you down here.' She had a deep strong voice which contrasted with the thin piping tones of Miss Aitken.

'What can I do for you?' I asked.

'It's these two,' she replied, pointing to a young couple immediately behind her. 'They want to get married in your church.'

'I think they had better come to the Vicarage with me now and I'll see if it can be arranged,' I said. I left my half-eaten biscuit on the plate and ushered the unexpected visitors from the hall in complete silence. As I closed the door I could hear an explosion of excited comments among the ladies, who would be talking about this intrusion into their meeting for days to come.

Once we were outside I said to the tongue-tied couple, 'I shall want to speak to the two of you on your own.'

'That's all right, Reverend,' replied the matriarch on their behalf. 'The rest of us have things to do. We'll see you back on the common when the Reverend has finished with you.'

As I walked to the Vicarage with the prospective bride and groom, I tried several times to get them to talk, only to elicit a string of monosyllables. They were not long out of adolescence by their appearance. The young man was neatly attired in a black suit, with a red scarf tied around his neck. His fiancée was a pretty young lady, in a long black dress which reached her open-toed sandals. By the time they were seated in my study, I had discovered that their names were Joe and Bridget and that they had been in the encampment on Abergelly Common for the past six months. Having established their residential qualification for marriage in the parish church, I began to take the details for the calling of banns. Joe's full name was Joseph Duffy and Bridget's was Bridget Palmer. Both were eighteen years old.

'That means that I shall have to have your parents' written consent,' I told them. They looked at each other.

'Will it be all right if they come here and tell you, instead of writing?' asked Bridget.

'That will do,' I replied. 'I shall write out a consent form and all they have to do is sign it.'

'Will I have to sign anything?' enquired Joe.

'Only the marriage register at your wedding,' I said.

His face dropped. 'I can't read or write,' he replied.

'Don't worry, Joe,' I assured him. 'It will be sufficient if you make a cross in the register.'

We arranged that their parents would come to the Vicarage on Friday evening and that the wedding would take place in six weeks' time. As they left, Mrs Cooper appeared from the kitchen. 'I hope you didn't mind me sending them down to the church hall,' she said. 'They wanted to stay here till you came. So it was a case of Robson's choice.'

When I was a Curate, my landlady, Mrs Richards, used to refer to 'Dobson's choice'. Eleanor remarked when I told her of the malapropism later that evening, 'I prefer Dobson to Robson if there's to be a choice.'

4

'For heaven's sake, Frederick,' ordered my wife. 'Pull yourself together, you are not facing a firing squad. Gareth Morgan is due to be in that position in half an hour's time, when you are supposed to be firing the bullets.'

'I think I'll pour myself a stiff whisky,' I said.

'No, you don't!' she replied. 'There is no need for you to be smelling of spirits when he arrives. Surely, as a man of God, you should be full of a different kind of spirit. He has been acting very foolishly as well as deviously as far as his wife is concerned. Tonight has to be the crunch for him.'

'The trouble is that he is such a nice bloke,' I murmured, 'the very last person you would think would do something like this.'

'You will soon find out how nice he really is,' went on Eleanor, 'when you broach the subject.'

This remark made me all the more nervous as I waited for the arrival of my churchwarden. How I wished that I had never developed a taste for Gilbert and Sullivan. I went into my study and sat at my desk, my head in my hands. Five minutes later there was a ring on the doorbell. I stood up, my heart pounding, and made my way slowly to open the front door.

'Ah, Vicar,' boomed the big man. 'What a lovely evening. It was a real treat to walk down from the hill, instead of taking the bus.'

I ushered the smiling Romeo into my study. 'Take a seat, Gareth,' I said, indicating an empty armchair at the side of my desk. I sat behind it in magisterial fashion. I took a deep breath. 'Before we talk about matters concerning St David's, as I indicated in my note to you, there is one other matter I want to bring up and that is your relationship with Janice Walters.'

His face went white and his head went down.

'It has been brought to my attention that you have formed some kind of attachment with this young school-girl. When I called on your wife some time earlier this week she told me that you were helping Hugh Thomas that evening in the youth club. When I called in at the club Hugh informed me that you have not been doing anything of the sort. Now, you may have been meeting her secretly.'

Suddenly he rose to his feet. By now his face was crimson with rage.

'Are you conducting some kind of witch hunt, Vicar?' he shouted. 'What I do with my private life is no concern of yours. All of a sudden an innocent friendship with this young lady has become some sordid affair. You can keep St David's and your Gilbert and Sullivan Society. That's it!' He strode out of the room and was through the front door before I had time to get from behind my desk and the magisterial chair.

By now Eleanor had emerged from the kitchen where she had been chatting with Mrs Cooper. 'That was a short and explosive interview,' she remarked as I came out from the study.

'So much for my stand as a man of God!' I exclaimed. 'He has finished with St David's and the G and S.'

'So much for the nice bloke,' said my wife. 'What did he have to say for himself?'

'He accused me of conducting some kind of a witch hunt over an innocent friendship with the young lady,' I said. 'So where do we go from here?'

'Where does he go from here?' she riposted. 'He has to explain to his wife why he has finished with St David's and the G and S. It will require a great deal of ingenuity on his part to provide an innocent explanation. At least he is aware that his indiscretion is now out in the open. I suppose the only other thing you can do is to have a word with the girl's parents.'

'Perhaps I should have done that before I talked to him on the subject,' I said. 'I shall have to get her address from one of the girls when they turn up for choir practice tomorrow.'

'How on earth are you going to do that if Janice is there?' replied my wife. 'They will ask you why on earth you don't ask her yourself.'

'In that case I shall have to get it from Graham Webb,' I suggested. 'It's just as well that he knows what has been going on. Perhaps I could have a word with him when he comes for his pre-practice meal.'

'I should think that is a much better idea than asking one of the girls,' said Eleanor. 'It may be that he has heard something which you don't know.' We decided that this would be the best policy under the circumstances.

When Graham arrived at the Vicarage the next afternoon in his new Morris Minor, he gave the impression that he was not exactly full of enthusiasm for his new undertaking.

'What a day,' he moaned, as he stood at the Vicarage door. 'Six hours of uninterested children to cope with and a pile of ill-informed homework to mark. I can only hope that St Peter's choir will be much better, though I am bound to say I doubt it.'

'What you need, Graham,' I said, 'is something inside your stomach to compensate for the lack of brain fodder. What about some pork chops and accessories washed down with a glass of bitter?'

'Vicar,' he replied, 'you have restored my faith in human nature.'

As we sat at the table, I broached the subject of Gareth Morgan's 'innocent friendship' with Janice Walters.

'I should have mentioned this before,' he said. 'A fortnight or so before the performance of *Pirates* I went outside the church hall for a smoke in the interval and I caught them kissing somewhat passionately. I had no idea that Gareth was married but I thought the age difference was significant. Furthermore, Janice was one of my pupils. Evidently I should have brought it to your attention. They were so absorbed in themselves that they did not notice my appearance. I realize now, after what you have said to me, that it was a stupid lapse on my part that I did not mention it to you.'

'Better late than never,' I replied. 'I should be very grateful if you would get her address for me.'

'Why on earth ask Graham to get the address?' intervened my wife. 'After what he has told us, why not get it from Ivor Hodges? Surely he should be made aware of what is happening, as her headmaster? I expect he will be there tonight, especially since he knows that Graham is taking over.'

'Quite right, Dr Secombe,' he said. 'It was a dereliction on my part as far as my headmaster and the Vicar are concerned that I did not report the incident. I suppose I was so concerned with the rehearsal that it went out of my mind. It certainly puts paid to Gareth's assertion that it was an "innocent relationship". By the way, Vicar, after what you have said about your encounter with him, I doubt very much if Janice will be there this evening, I expect he has got word to her that you know of the liaison.'

He was right, Janice was conspicuous by her absence at the choir practice. All the other girls were there making 'a joyful noise unto the Lord'. What would have been a very happy occasion was spoilt for me by the knowledge that I had a potentially disastrous situation on my hands. Graham had played the organ in a way that I had not heard before, with a competence which transformed the instrument. The new recruits had give the impression that St Peter's church choir was worthy of a prominent position in the valleys' choral league. Bill Ace, tenor of thirty years' standing, made the comment that the chancel had never echoed to such singing in his lifetime.

Ivor Hodges, beaming with pride at the contribution his school had made, said, 'I shan't compete with Bill's poetic tribute but I will say that I can see a bright future for our parish church in the field of music.' Then he turned to me. 'Vicar, you don't seem to be all that happy. What's wrong?'

'I am perfectly happy with the practice,' I replied, 'but there is something not connected with the music that you and I must have a talk about. If you have a few minutes to spare, perhaps you would come with me to the Vicarage.'

We went into the sitting room where Eleanor was watching a programme on television. 'Sorry to interrupt your viewing, love. I didn't know you were in here,' I explained.

'Not to worry,' she replied. 'I can switch off and do something useful in the kitchen, like preparing for tomorrow's dinner.'

'Don't do that,' I said. 'I think you had better stay where you are while I tell Ivor about the Gareth Morgan saga. After all, you are party to the G and S set-up.'

Ivor looked puzzled. 'Sit down,' I went on, 'and all will be revealed.' He sat on the settee alongside my wife and I ensconced myself in my favourite armchair.

'I'm afraid that you will not be pleased with what I have to tell you. It appears that an affair has developed between Gareth and Janice Walters. When I first heard rumours about it, I was prepared to dismiss them. I thought that Gareth was not that kind of man. However, since then I have found out that he was telling his wife that he had been spending his time helping Hugh Thomas with the youth club when he was not near the place. Now this evening Graham has told us that he saw the two of them in a passionate embrace outside the church hall. I have charged Gareth with these accusations. He vehemently denied them and has resigned from his post as churchwarden and as a member of the G and S Society. It would seem that the only course left to me is to inform Janice's parents about the whole affair.'

Ivor sat silent for a while. He looked stunned. Eventually he said quietly, 'I would never have thought that he would have been so stupid as to involve himself in a love affair with a schoolgirl. As you say, so far his wife is not aware of what is happening. That is something.'

'What I should like to do, Ivor,' I replied, 'is to go to the girl's parents and tell them about the situation. If you could give me their address, I shall go and see them next Monday, or at least see her mother, if her father is at work.'

'That won't be necessary,' said Ivor. 'Her mother is a widow and she will be devastated when she finds out what is happening. Janice has been a good daughter to her. That makes Gareth's behaviour all the more reprehensible. Why in God's name should he be so irresponsible?'

On hearing this I had never felt so angry in all my life. Eleanor turned to Ivor. 'Is this a one-off or has it happened before since you have been head of the school?' she asked.

'We have had two fifteen-year-old mothers and three sixteen-year-olds who have been pregnant,' he replied. 'Strangely enough, the seventeen-year-olds and the eighteen-year-olds have not given us any trouble on that account.'

'Let's hope that Janice comes into that category,' said my wife.

'Well, if you can pass on that address, I shall call on Mrs Walters next Monday afternoon,' I told my churchwarden. 'Now then, to much more pleasant matters. How do you think the talent scheme will blossom next Sunday?'

'From what I can gather, Vicar,' he said, 'you are in for a big surprise. Apparently Dai Elbow's greyhound had another win on Tuesday.' Dai had used his pound to bet on his bitch, Della. As he put it, the Almighty had changed his no-hoper into the queen of the track in the valleys.

'The knitting brigade have been hard at work. Half of our school cricket team have been supplied with pullovers and that is just from Esme Jones, our next-door neighbour. There's no doubt that this idea has caught the imagination of the congregation. Marion, Gareth's wife, has been doing pencil drawings of St Peter's.'

'I wonder if she will be at the parish church on Sunday,' I said to him. 'I don't know what he is going to do to explain his resignation to her.'

'At the moment,' suggested Eleanor, 'probably nothing. I should think he will develop a severe headache or a stomach complaint to excuse his absence from church on Sunday. He will need a few days to work out a strategy to cover his tracks. I would expect Marion to be at the service with the proceeds of her sales.'

'I'm sure you are right,' agreed Ivor. 'The longer he can keep his indiscretion from his wife the better, as far as he is concerned. We can only hope that he does that long enough to give time for Mrs Walters to speak to her daughter.'

When I made my way down the church path for the talent service on Sunday, it was a gloriously sunny morning. An excited crowd had gathered outside the porch. In the midst of them was Dai Elbow plus his racing champion, the centre of attention among the worshippers.

'I've brought Della with me, Vic,' said Dai. 'I'm sure you won't mind me bringing 'er. After all, it's 'er that's multiplied the talent, isn't it? I thought I'd bring 'er up to the altar when we all take our gifts. I'll see that she behaves 'erself.'

At that stage in the conversation the photographer from the *Monmouth Gazette* intervened. 'Can I have a photograph of you together with the Vicar?' he asked. Against a background of spectators eagerly responding to the 'cheese' request from behind the camera, the picture was taken, later to hang in the vestry.

The new female choristers had been kitted out on Friday evening and were parading outside the chancel door when I arrived to vest for the Communion service. Graham Webb was enjoying himself at the organ with Bach's Toccata and Fugue in D minor. Hugh Thomas had caught the mood. His face was split by a wide smile as he came to meet me.

'This is going to be red-letter day in the history of St Peter's,' he proclaimed. 'The church is three-quarters full already and there's still a quarter of an hour to go. What a treat to hear such inspiring music from the organist and to see such a large choir. I know it's sad to lose Evan Roberts, but the old order giveth place to new. "The Lord hath given and the Lord hath taken away. Blessed be the name of the Lord."'

'I don't think Mrs Roberts would agree with those sentiments,' I replied. 'As far as she is concerned, St Peter's will never be the same without him. That is quite true and time will tell. I trust it will tell a much more inspiring story. We shall see.'

By the time the choir and clergy proceeded into the church to the strains of 'The Church's one foundation', sung with such fervour that I felt that the building would be in need of renovations as a result, I became convinced that the parish of Abergelly had come alive and that the Lord was gracious unto Sion. As the service progressed and the sense of dedication became apparent among the congregation, I went up into the pulpit to preach my sermon.

'First of all,' I said, 'I must pay tribute to Evan Roberts who for so many years has been the organist and choirmaster of the parish church. His sudden demise reminds us of the sentence from the burial service that "in the midst of life we are in death". Our heartfelt sympathy must go to his widow and her family. I am sure that he would have been thrilled to see such a full church at this dedication of our talents to our Lord and Master in Abergelly. We are grateful to Mr Graham Webb who has undertaken to serve as organist and choirmaster in the emergency and, we trust, to carry on in the same dedicated manner as his predecessor, using his undoubted talent in tune with the theme of today, if I may say so. Each one of you who will be bringing your gifts to the altar this morning has dedicated your talent, whatever it may be, to the Giver of all good gifts.'

At that point in my sermon there came a loud high-pitched yelp from the talented greyhound, to the great amusement of most of the congregation but to the obvious embarrassment of Dai Elbow, who decided to take Della out before she could cause any further interruption. Unfortunately, in his haste to remove the animal both of them came into contact with the legs of Tom Beynon, the people's warden, who was in his accustomed seat at the end of the pew. This resulted in Dai sprawling in the aisle surmounted by a continuing yelping dog. By the time the two of them had made their exit I had decided to bring my potentially inspiring address to an abrupt end. Like actors, preachers can never compete successfully with animals or children.

When the moment arrived for the presentation of the multiplied talents at the altar, Dai made a solo appearance. Behind him, to my great relief, was a smiling Marion Morgan.

As I stood outside the porch to shake hands with the congregation, Marion informed me that Gareth had been laid low with a bad migraine. 'It's years since he has had an attack,' she told me.

'Any more like that,' I said to her, 'and you will have to see the doctor.'

Dai Elbow accused Tom Beynon of accidentally putting his foot on Della's paw. 'She would have been fine if it wasn't for that. Then, of course, if he stood up when I was taking the dog out instead of sitting down, we would not have fallen over his legs. There you are, that's 'ow it goes. The great thing is the money you are going to 'ave when it's counted. That's what matters. You are in for a big surprise.'

'Where is Della now?' I asked him.

'I've put 'er in the car. She was fast asleep there when I looked just now. If it 'adn't been for Tom, she would 'ave been as good as gold.'

I could not get to the vestry quickly enough to watch the opening of the envelopes by the churchwardens. 'Sorry I trod on Della's paw,' said Tom Beynon as I came through the door. 'She's got such long legs, you see, Vicar, and since I've got such big feet I suppose something was bound to happen. Anyway, let's get down to business. We've counted the collection. That was five pounds and ten shillings up on last Sunday. Ivor's got the checksheet ready by here with the names of those who had the talents given to them.'

'Are you sitting comfortably, Vicar?' said his fellow churchwarden as I sat in my chair by the side of the desk. I nodded my head vigorously. 'Then we'll begin.' I was joined by Hugh Thomas who had sacrificed his midday rendezvous with his beloved to savour the excitement of the occasion.

'Let's get Dai Elbow's envelope opened first,' suggested Ivor. 'It's absolutely bulging.'

'I vote for that,' proclaimed my Curate. Tom's fingers trembled as he tried to open the envelope.

'For God's sake, don't tear the notes,' warned Ivor.

'I think you had better do it,' said his fellow warden. 'I don't want to make confetti out of it.'

Gingerly the envelope was opened, and a wad of notes was spread out on the desk. Fivers and ten-pound notes mingled with the humble pound variety.

'One hundred and seven pounds,' announced Ivor.

'Fantastic!' shouted Hugh.

One by one the envelopes were opened, including one for twenty-seven pounds from Marion Morgan, another from the Mothers' Union with thirty-two pounds from their combined knitting effort and another from Jim James, who had raised thirty-five pounds by doing odd jobs in Abergelly. Others included five pounds, six shillings and tuppence from Bernard Williams, a choirboy at St Peter's, who had made small toys out of felt; eight pounds and fifteen shillings from old Mrs Baldwin, whose daughter had sold her Welsh cakes at the weekly Abergelly market, and many others in the same category of doing little things with the talent they had possessed.

When the total of money raised was finally counted it came to nine hundred and eighty-seven pounds and ten-pence.

'Since my wife and I have not taken part in the scheme,' I said, 'we shall give another twenty pounds to bring it over the thousand mark.'

'That is splendid,' remarked Ivor. 'I know Tom's wife and mine have raised a reasonable amount. Dr Secombe has enough to do without being involved in something like this, and don't forget that there are still nine talents outstanding. All in all, this has been a great success and it will bring us a little closer to the target we shall have to obtain if we are to match the Earl of Duffryn's contribution to a new church at Brynfelin.'

'I am afraid, Ivor,' I replied, 'that today's effort is a good deal short of that target. There are only eight more years to go. This is only the beginning. Much more ingenuity and much more sacrifice will be necessary if that church is to become a reality.'

At that stage in the conversation Hugh Thomas intervened. 'As the priest who is in charge of Brynfelin, may I say how vital it is that a new building, a permanent one, is built on the estate. It will have to be a multi-purpose one since the people there have no social centre. If it comes to that, they have no shops. They have been dumped there. I know Dr Secombe's doing a tremendous job as a doctor but they have to become a community. Otherwise, as the years go by there will be a tremendous rise in crime among the young people, whose lives will become completely aimless, I can assure you.'

'Thank you, Hugh, for that contribution,' I replied. 'I can only hope that you will stay long enough in the parish to create a sense of community on the estate. If the Council would give us a house as a parsonage, that would be a step forward.'

'I don't see why not,' said Ivor. 'After all, Dr Secombe was allowed the use of a house for her surgery. What is a parsonage but an ecclesiastical surgery? People's souls are just as important as their bodies.'

'Why on earth did you say we would give twenty pounds?' demanded Eleanor when I told her of my pledge in the vestry.

'I think it is the least we can do,' I replied indignantly.

'So do I!' she said. 'It should be fifty pounds as a minimum. When you think of all the money coming into this house compared with the average wage in the parish, twenty pounds is a derisory amount. I say that we should give a hundred pounds, and even that would be short of Dai Elbow's contribution.'

'Fine,' I replied. 'My trouble is that I was brought up in a council house where a hundred pounds would be considered a small fortune.'

'For heaven's sake, Frederick,' she riposted, 'stop playing that old violin again. Sometimes I think you are suffering from a massive inferiority complex. I can't give you any medicine for that. You have to be your own physician to deal with a problem which is peculiar to yourself.' Then she put her arms around me, lifted up my head and kissed me. 'Dinner is served,' she said. 'Let's join the family for one of Mrs Cooper's five-star meals, roast beef, roast potatoes, Yorkshire pudding and one of Tom Beynon's home-grown cauliflowers. What more could you ask?' We went into the dining room with our arms around each other.

'Dad?' said my son plaintively. 'Can we go out in the car this afternoon, with Lulu?'

'You know full well that you are supposed to be going to Sunday school,' I replied. 'What is Miss Bevan going to say when she finds that you are not in her class? The Vicar's son going out in the car to take the dog for a walk on a Sunday afternoon?'

'Auntie Cooper said that Lulu hasn't been out for a walk today because you and Mummy have been busy and I thought that perhaps we could take her out 'cos she's been in all day.'

David's plea was supported apologetically by our housekeeper. 'I'm sorry, Vicar,' she said, 'I don't want to interfere, but Lulu has been stuck in her basket all this morning. If you or Dr Secombe could take her out that's fine, but I thought it would be nice if David could have a ticket to leave, as they say, just for today.'

'Can I come too?' came the wheedling tones of Elspeth.

I looked at Eleanor. 'What do you say, Mother?' I said, attempting a North-country accent.

'I must say that was a pathetic Stanley Holloway impersonation,' she replied, 'but in answer to your question, yes, children, let's have a Sunday afternoon off for a change.'

'Hooray!' shouted David. Elspeth clapped her hands, and Mrs Cooper looked relieved that her 'ticket to leave' had been granted without any resentment at her intrusion into family affairs.

As soon as our Sunday dinner was over, we collected an excited Lulu from her basket and made our way to our old Ford 8. The two children were fighting for the dog's attention on the back seat and Eleanor had made herself comfortable alongside me as the front passenger when the gates of the drive were thrown open and a distraught Marion Morgan appeared.

'You take over, love,' I said to my wife. 'It looks as if I have a long afternoon ahead of me.'

5

'I've spoiled your outing,' said a tearful Marion Morgan as I led her into my study.

'Of course not,' I replied. 'We were only going to take the dog for a walk on the Mynydd mountains. Take a seat in that armchair.'

I carried the chair from behind my desk and sat down alongside her. She began to sob bitterly. I put my arm around her. I let her cry until she could cry no more. 'I'm sorry, Vicar,' she managed to say between gulps.

'I'll get you something to drink and then you can tell me why you are so upset,' I replied. I went into the sitting room and poured her half a tumbler of whisky and soda. She sat bent with her head bowed and taking an occasional sip from the glass. It seemed an eternity before she could bring herself to speak. Then she raised her head and looked me in the eyes.

'Gareth has left me.' Her voice was flat, dead, devoid of feeling. 'He has left me for a schoolgirl, Janice Walters. They have gone away together. When I got home from church, there was a letter on the table. He had put it up against the vase of flowers I had bought yesterday to celebrate our wedding anniversary, which is tomorrow. That was cruel. He said he was very sorry but that he did not love me any more and that he was deeply in love with this girl and she was with him. Where they have gone I do not know. Her parents must be beside themselves. I feel so ashamed that my husband could have done this to them. Vicar, what can I do? What can I do?' She stressed each word of that last sentence.

I took a deep breath. 'First of all, Marion, I have to tell you that I found out about this relationship a week ago. When I called at your home last Monday, I was hoping to see him there. When you told me that he had gone down to St David's to help Hugh Thomas with the youth club, I called in. He was not there. Not only that, he had never been helping Hugh at the club. As a result, I sent him a note asking him to come and see me. When I broached the subject of Janice Walters, he was annoyed and told me that he would resign as warden. He said I should not interfere in his private life and stormed out of the Vicarage. There's one other thing – you talked about Janice's parents. Her father is dead. She is the only child of her widowed mother.'

When I told her this, her face went white. Her voice shook with anger and she replied. 'That is the end. How could he do such a thing? We have been married for six happy years. We were going to start a family next year, once we had enough money behind us. As far as I know he has never looked at another woman. Our sex life was very satisfying. Everything was going for us. That girl's mother must be devastated. To lose her husband was bad enough, but to lose her daughter when she was still at school! I shall have to go and see her.'

'Ivor Hodges is giving me her address tomorrow morning,' I said. 'I shall be paying her a visit, once I know where she lives. Would you like to come with me or would you prefer to go on your own?'

'Thank you, Vicar,' she replied, 'but I'd rather be with her on my own, woman to woman.'

'In that case,' I went on, 'I'll slip a note through your door once I have had the information from Ivor.'

'You won't have to do that,' she said, 'I shall be in. I can't go to work at a time like this. I'll be going to my mother down in Newport from here for the rest of the day, but I'll be back at home later tonight. There's a bus due in the square at half past three. If I leave now I'll be able to catch it. What she is going to say when I tell her what has happened I hate to think. You see, she never liked Gareth. All I hope is that she won't start reminding me about that. I'm afraid I won't be able to take it.'

She stood up and held her hand out. I took it and she held mine in a tight grip for quite a while before releasing it. By now she had regained her composure. 'Thank you, Vicar, for your help. I'll see you tomorrow morning.'

I saw her to the door and watched her stride up the drive, with her shoulders back and her head held high. She was a different woman from the broken reed who came through the gate earlier on.

No sooner had I returned to the house when the phone announced its presence. It was the Rural Dean. As he began to speak it was obvious that he was in an advanced state of perturbation.

'Vicar, I – er – wonder if – er – you can help out in an urgent case, as it were. The Rector of – er – Pentwyn has been suddenly, as it were, struck down with a heart attack just a few hours ago. He has an evening Communion fixed for 6.30 p.m. If it was – er – Evensong, the lay reader could have filled the bill, shall we say. Now that you have the usefulness of a Curate who has been made a priest at the last ordination, I wonder perhaps if you could show your willingness to let him take the service.'

Henry Jones, Vicar of Pentwyn, was an eccentric churchman. I had no wish to expose Hugh Thomas so early in his priesthood to what might confront him in St Dyfrig's, the parish church.

'I'm sorry to hear that the Rector has suffered a heart attack, Mr Rural Dean,' I said. 'I hope it is not too serious. As for the service this evening, I shall take it and leave my Curate to preside at Evensong here in Abergelly.'

'That's very kind of you, Vicar,' he replied. 'You have lifted a burden off my mind, shall I say. You know what it is like to get, how shall I put it – er – spur of the moment helping out. Thank you once again for being so willing to be the Good Samaritan, as it were. Oh, by the way, I did enjoy your er play at the Welfare Hall a fortnight ago about the Pirates of Penzance, very good it was.'

Half an hour later, Eleanor arrived with three seated companions, two children and a dog. While David and Elspeth rushed into the kitchen to tell Auntie Cooper about their adventures on Mynydd Mountain, Eleanor came into the study followed by a leaping Lulu, who had to be consigned to her basket in the garage before we could hold a conversation.

'Now then,' gasped my wife after her exertions with the Vicarage hound, 'let's have an account of the Marion

Morgan episode.' She slumped in the chair previously occupied by the said lady.

'Well, I'm afraid it is not a pretty story, believe me. In short, Gareth Morgan has run off with Janice Walters. When Marion arrived home she found a letter informing her that he was in love with Janice and she was with him and that they were going away together. To make matters worse, the letter was propped against a vase containing flowers Marion had bought to celebrate their wedding anniversary, which is tomorrow.'

'The swine!' exploded my wife. 'Excuse the language, but that's the only word for him. What about that girl's poor mother, a widow, with an only child. So much for the decent chap you thought he was. Come to think of it, he has a loose mouth. I'm not talking about his language, which was always circumspect, but about his physiognomy. Poor Marion must be shattered. She looked terrible as we passed her on the drive.'

'She was a different person when she left here,' I said. 'Once she had cried out her grief, she recovered her composure and strode up the drive with her shoulders back and her head held high.'

'Not many women in her position could have done that,' replied Eleanor. 'She must have tremendous strength of character and she'll certainly need it in the months that lie ahead of her. I wonder how long this romance will last. I would think that all the glamour would wear off quickly for Janice if they have to share a bedsit somewhere and then search for some menial job to pay the rent. Life won't be so attractive then.'

By the time we had finished discussing the Gareth

Morgan escapade it was five o'clock. 'What about a nice cup of tea and a sandwich?' I said.

'What's the hurry?' asked my wife.

'I had an urgent SOS from our friend the Rural Dean,' I replied, 'just after Marion Morgan left. Henry Jones at Pentwyn has had a heart attack and he wanted Hugh Thomas to take the evening Communion service. I could not inflict Hugh with the prospect of presiding at one of Henry's way-out extravaganzas with Ribena as a substitute for wine and the Sankey and Moody choruses to Communion hymns. It's the Curate's task to preach at Evensong here. I am sure he will not mind the extra duty of taking the service.'

'Henry Jones, that fat old gentleman with a big red nose?' enquired Eleanor. I nodded. 'I would have thought that he had acquired that proboscis via the whisky bottle, rather than doses of Ribena. How wrong can you be!'

'It isn't often one hears a doctor admit she was wrong in diagnosis,' I said.

'We are all human,' replied my wife.

St Dyfrig's church, Pentwyn, was a small medieval building which had been extensively renovated in the last century. A plain wooden altar unadorned by a frontal cross or candles stood against the east wall, which was disfigured by a garish enumeration of the Ten Commandments painted by a third-rate artist of bygone years. Three of them had fallen prey to the damp which had invaded the plaster, removing theft, adultery and murder from the forbidden list. On the north end of the 'holy table' was the lectern bearing the service book, and at its foot a decidedly uncomfortable stool, a most uninviting prospect for the celebrant.

I had arrived at 6.15 p.m. to be greeted by an elderly lady who informed me that she was the Vicar's warden. There were half a dozen people in the congregation. In the vestry, the chalice and paten were on the table. The chalice was three-quarters full of a red liquid. I tasted it. 'Definitely a vintage Ribena,' I said to myself. A few minutes later, a bald-headed red-faced gentleman came in with a small brown paper bag.

'Thank you, Vicar, for helping us out. I am Daniel Williams, the lay reader. I've brought the bread for the service.' He emptied the cubes cut from the slice of a loaf on to the paten. 'Two days old,' he went on. 'Much easier to cut then. Here are the hymns for this evening. Miss Owen, our organist, hasn't turned up yet. It may be that she thinks the service is cancelled because of the Vicar's heart attack. If she doesn't come I'll give you the note on the harmonium so that you can start us off.'

'Wait a minute, Mr Williams,' I replied. 'I understand that you do not use *Hymns Ancient and Modern* but some kind of mission hymn book. If that is the case, I am afraid that I will not know the tunes.'

'I'll bring you the book now,' he said. 'If you do not know the tunes of the ones picked for this evening, perhaps we can have a look to see if you know some of the other ones.'

As he spoke there was a tap on the door. It was Miss Owen, a diminutive lady with pince-nez on the large nose which dominated her small face.

'Good evening, Vicar,' she said in a high fluting voice. 'I see you have the hymn list. We sing the responses but say the psalm. We do sing the Magnificat and the Nunc Dimittis. I will give you the note for the responses.'

I breathed a sigh of relief as she left the vestry. I had no desire to lead unaccompanied singing of mission hymns.

'Shall I put the chalice and paten on the holy table, Vicar?' enquired the lay reader.

'Yes, please,' I replied. 'By the way, would you move the stool from the end of the altar? I am afraid I shall feel very uneasy trying to kneel on it, so I shall stand.'

'If you don't mind me saying so,' said David Williams, 'our Vicar kneels on it and he's a lot older than you.'

'Maybe, Mr Williams,' I snapped, 'but he is used to kneeling on the thing and I am not. I don't want to have an attack of cramp halfway through the proceedings. So for this once, I am afraid you will have to put up with a standing celebrant.' He muttered to himself as he took the vessels into the sanctuary. I could make out the words 'High Church' as part of his soliloquy.

From the volume of sound coming from the nave, it was evident that the half-dozen in the congregation had been multiplied by at least three or four times. As the warden of my theological college would say, they were 'far too much at ease in Sion. A church is not a concert hall, gentlemen.' There was a subdued murmur from the worshippers at my churches in Pontywen and Abergelly prior to a service. Here in Pentwyn it sounded like a football match. I looked at my wristwatch. It was exactly six thirty. I said the vestry prayer very loudly and went out of the vestry.

In the nave of the church the conversation continued unabated in its decibels. Some people were sitting, others were standing and a few were wandering around. As I stood at the north end of the altar, appalled at the chaos in front of me, I bellowed in tones of which a sergeant major would have been proud, 'QUIET!' There was an instant reaction. They froze into silent statues.

'Would you all be seated, please,' I ordered. The peripatetic few found the nearest vacant chair and a deadly hush ensued. Suddenly I became aware that I was in somebody else's church and that I had no right to treat the congregation as if they were unruly children. Evidently it was their custom to behave like that. I swallowed hard as I realized the extent of my audacity.

'As you are all aware,' I said quietly, 'your Rector has been laid low with a heart attack. The Rural Dean has asked me to take the Communion service this evening. We shall pray for the Rector in the prayers for the sick. I hope you will put up with me because I am not familiar with your form of worship.' I looked at the hymn list. 'We shall commence by singing hymn number 217,' I announced. There was a silence, during which Miss Owen kept looking at me. It dawned on me that they were accustomed to having the first verse read out to them. I obliged and spoke of the need to be washed in the blood of the Lamb. The hymn may not have been to my liking, but I had to admire the full-throated singing which followed.

I decided to give my address from the chancel step instead of the pulpit which was tucked away on the south side of the church. Halfway through my peroration there was a heavy thunder shower and water began to drip copiously on my head. I moved to one side to avoid any further contact with the rain but it seemed to follow me as I went, to the great amusement of my listeners, who must have thought that I was being put in my place by the

Almighty. My address ended abruptly. As I went to the altar during the next hymn three buckets were placed by the lay reader and the churchwardens to catch the rain water. For the rest of the service my voice had to compete with the musical trio of the buckets.

My administration of the sacrament was punctuated with 'thank you's from the communicants, with an occasional 'thank you very much' thrown in. Evidently they were fond of Ribena because the last three worshippers had to be content with a few beads of liquid left in the chalice. I was met with a hostile stare as they realized they had been cheated of their usual gulp of liquid. After the service was over the churchwardens came into the vestry to count the collection. The people's warden, an elderly gentleman bent with age and apparently even older than his female counterpart, said that the last few communicants had complained that they were given an empty chalice.

'It's my fault,' came a voice from the doorway. It was the lay reader bringing back the chalice and paten from the altar. 'The Vicar always keeps a bottle of Ribena on the side table. I forgot to put it out, what with all the upheaval and that.'

What he meant by 'that' I shall never know. I was only too eager to make my escape from St Dyfrig's as soon as possible. When I left, the congregation was still occupying the nave in little clusters of gossipers. Not a head was turned as I made my departure. It was one of those occasions when someone was made to feel very much *persona non grata*. I suppose that my shouted request for silence made that inevitable.

As I got into my car there was a blinding flash of lightning in the pitch black sky. Then the heavens opened and I drove back to Abergelly in a deluge which overwhelmed the windscreen wipers. I pulled into the side entertained by thunder rolls and a display of pyrotechnics worthy of any performance of Tchaikovsky's '1812' Overture. I thought of the scene in St Dyfrig's chancel where the buckets would have been overflowing. The church was one of a number in the valley which had been affected by mining subsidence. Evidently, the chancel and the nave were in danger of parting company. Should poor Henry Jones not recover from his heart attack, his successor would be confronted with the enormous task of restoring this ancient church. With a dwindling congregation and a yearly income just sufficient to pay running expenses, the new incumbent would deserve the George Cross if he could achieve its rescue. My task of building the new church in the Brynfelin estate no longer looked Herculean in comparison.

Almost miraculously, the storm abated and the evening sun bathed the valley in its rose-red light. I switched on the engine and made my way back to the Vicarage in buoyant mood, singing loudly 'The day Thou gavest, Lord, has ended'.

Eleanor met me as I came through the door. 'You have a visitor,' she said, 'Janice Walters' mother. Sorry, love, that you have to be inflicted with a second dose of Garethitis in the space of a few hours. She is very distressed. I have tried to calm her, with little success, I am afraid. I have taken her into the sitting room. I'll try some tea and biscuits later on.'

A smartly dressed lady in her early forties, it would appear, was seated in an armchair by the window. She was dabbing her eyes with a lace handkerchief. As I entered the room she stood up and burst into tears. In a repeat of the Marion Morgan episode I put my arm around her and led her back into the armchair.

'Please sit down, Mrs Walters,' I said. 'I am so sorry about what has happened, and anything that I can do to help, I shall do.' I was about to say 'I shall be pleased to do' and bit my tongue as I realized that there was no pleasure involved. I waited for the tears to subside.

'You must excuse me, Vicar,' she murmured. 'I am normally quite self-controlled but this is something so unexpected and totally out of character for Janice and it has bowled me over.' Her accent did not belong to the valleys, neither did her mode of expression.

'She has been such a good girl,' she went on, 'very caring, especially when my late husband died of cancer four years ago. Without her, I don't know what I would have done at that time. At school, she has been most conscientious in her work. Her teacher said that she had every chance of getting three good A levels. In fact she was too conscientious. That's why I was so glad that she had joined your Gilbert and Sullivan Society. She was so happy when she did. She loves singing and enjoyed her acting bit. She was looking forward to being in *The Mikado*. She began to weep again.

After a few more dabs at her eyes she resumed her monologue. 'You see, I had three A levels when I was at school in Northampton and I used to take part in all the school plays. Then the war came and I ended up in the

WAAFS, that's where I met my husband. He was a leading aircraftsman at the aerodrome where I was stationed. When the war was over we got married and came back to Abergelly. We had Janice straight away. It was a caesarean and we were lucky that she lived. I could have no more children after than. She has been my pride and joy ever since. When my husband died I got a job in the factory where he was employed as a fitter. I am now the secretary to the managing director in Pontypool. I don't know why I am telling you all this. I suppose it is some kind of catharsis.'

'Cathartic or not,' I replied, 'if it helps you to keep a cool head, all well and good. Do you mind me asking if Janice left you a note or a letter of some kind?'

She delved into her handbag and handed me an envelope. 'Read it for yourself,' she said.

'My dear Mam,' it began, 'I don't know how to write this. I have fallen deeply in love with Gareth Morgan. He is a married man and years older than me. He has fallen madly in love with me. It seems that the only course open to us is to go away together. The Vicar has found out about us and has told Gareth that he must stop our relationship. We can't live without each other. So that's it, Mam. I love you so very much. I will let you know how things are once we have settled down together. I am so sorry to hurt you like this. It is the last thing on earth I want to do. Please forgive me. Your ever-loving daughter, Janice.'

Anything more different than the curt and cruel letter left for his wife by Gareth Morgan it would be difficult to find, I told Eleanor later. When I finished reading it I looked up and saw such pain in the mother's face that I turned away, unable to be a witness of its intensity.

'How do you cope with that?' she asked. There was a knock on the door and my wife came in with a tray of tea and biscuits to save me from a reply to an impossible question. I handed the letter back and moved a small table to the side of the armchair, where Eleanor deposited the tray.

'I hope you like your tea strong?' she said to Mrs Walters.

'The stronger the better, at a time like this,' she replied, 'and preferably with a dose of arsenic.'

'Come on,' replied my wife, 'don't talk like that. Arsenic would not solve anything and it would only make a bad situation worse.'

'I don't think it can be any worse than it is,' the widow rejoined. 'If only she had not joined your Society, this would never have happened – not that I'm blaming you, of course.'

I could see Eleanor's hackles rise. 'My dear Mrs Walters,' she said icily, 'it is not the Society which has caused the trouble, it is Janice's naivety. In any case there is no use in indulging in "ifs" and "onlys". Let's hope that she will soon see the futility of the situation in which she finds herself.' So saying, she made a swift exit.

'Oh dear,' said Janice's mother, 'I am afraid I have offended your wife. That is the last thing I want to do.'

'Please don't worry about that,' I assured her. 'You have enough to do coping with your daughter's disappearance. Eleanor has a quick temper and would not want to exacerbate matters. Drink your strong cup of tea and have a biscuit.'

'I'll drink the tea,' she said, 'but I don't want any biscuits, thank you. I have not eaten anything since I found that letter. It would stick in my throat.'

We sat in silence for a while, drinking the tea. Both of us had run out of words. I remember reading once in a book of extracts from the writings of the saints that silence had a healing quality which was God-given. Outside the room there came the sounds of David and Elspeth's voices as they were being taken up to bed. They added the picture of innocence to the mental climate which had settled on us since my wife's departure.

Eventually the widow drained her cup and stood up. 'Thank you, Vicar, I'll go back now. I have sat by the phone until eleven o'clock this morning until I came to see you. I asked my neighbour to come in and look after the house in case there was a call from Janice. I don't want to impose on her. How I am going to face going back to work tomorrow, wondering all day if the phone has rung, I don't know. Anyway, thank you once again for listening to me so sympathetically. I can only hope that your little girl does not give you the same heartache which Janice has given to me when she grows up.'

She held out her hand. It was a limp handshake compared to that which Marion Morgan had given me earlier in the day, neither did she stride up the drive as Gareth's wife had done. It was a forlorn little figure who made her way out of the Vicarage. As she went I realized that I should have told her that Marion was coming to see her tomorrow. Then I came to the conclusion that it was just as well that I had not done so. Gareth's wife was determined to comfort Janice's mother 'woman to woman' as she put it. That was something that no parish priest could do.

I closed the door. As I did so my wife came up behind me and put her arms around me. 'I'm sorry, love,' she said quietly, 'I shouldn't have spoken to that poor woman as I did. Sometimes I cannot believe that I can be so insensitive. For a doctor that is a grievous fault.'

'My dear Eleanor,' I replied, 'if you had seen the pain in her face when I looked up at her after reading her daughter's very moving letter, I am sure you would never be insensitive again. She is a devoted mother who has been deeply wounded by the one great love of her life. I tell you what, Marion Morgan will recover from this sad episode much more quickly than Mrs Walters. Gareth's selfish scribble to his wife is not in the same category as that girl's letter to her mother. He has blotted his copy-book for good.'

'Well, Frederick,' commented Eleanor, 'in the words of the song, "Little man, you've had a busy day". How did your safari to Pentwyn go, by the way?'

'I'll save up that saga for tomorrow, if you don't mind,' I said. 'Let's get to bed.'

'With pleasure,' she replied, and kissed me warmly.

6

Three weeks went by and nothing was heard from the runaway couple.

'I think the time has come to make Dai Elbow the new churchwarden at St David's,' I said to Eleanor. 'He has been opening up the church and counting the collection for the past three Sundays. He may as well have the right of being appointed churchwarden. I know Stan Richards was the key figure in the erection of the church but that's where his interest ended. He has only attended services up there two or three times since the place was opened. I don't think Dai has missed once. He was the most enthusiastic of the helpers during the construction work.'

'I tell you what,' replied my wife, 'his cup will be running over. He will be so proud. What's more, he thoroughly deserves the honour, if one may call it that.'

One who called it that was its recipient, who gave the word a heavily accentuated aspirate when I asked him if he would be my warden. 'All I 'ope is that I shall be worthy of the Honour,' he said.

'I think you will be an excellent churchwarden,' I told him.

Like Sir Joseph Porter in the libretto of *HMS Pinafore*, his bosom swelled with pride. 'Mind,' he went on to say, 'I'm sorry about Gareth, Vic. I never suspected about 'is goings on with that young girl. Marion must be going round the bend.'

'I don't think so, Dai,' I replied. 'She is just very angry, very angry indeed.'

We were in the parlour of Dai's semi-detached residence, 21 Aberdare Crescent, on a hillside overlooking Abergelly. He had come off his six to two shift at the colliery and was still in his overalls. The smell of liver and onions coming from the kitchen greeted me as he opened the door to me. As we stood looking down on the town through the bay window, there was a knock on the door. Menna Rees entered, wearing a pinafore and with her hair in curlers. She looked startled to see me.

'Sorry Vicar, I didn't know it was you here. I was going to tell Dai that his dinner was ready.'

'Wot do you think?' he said to his wife. 'I'm the new churchwarden at St David's.'

Her eyes opened wide and her jaw dropped. She was a little woman who was dwarfed by her rugby-playing husband. Despite the difference in physical stature, Menna was more than Dai's equal in every other respect. Slim, grey-haired and brown-eyed, she had a keen sense of humour.

'Well!' she exclaimed. 'What a turn up for the book! No more greyhound tracks for you, boyo. It's the straight and narrow from now on. What's more, you can drop the "Vic", David Rees. It's "Vicar", don't forget. That's right, isn't it, Vicar?' She gave me a wink, as Dai raised his eyes to the heavens.

'Not really,' I replied. 'I think Dai would miss the greyhound track as much as I would miss the "Vic".'

'Thank God for that!' said the new churchwarden.

'I had better be going,' I announced, 'otherwise your liver and onions will get cold and there's nothing worse than cold liver and onions. See you next Sunday, Dai.'

I thought I had better go in to see Hugh Thomas at the service to announce that Mr David Rees was now churchwarden at St David's. It would come as a surprise to some in the small congregation to know that Dai had a surname which was not 'Elbow'. Many years had passed since Dai Rees had been banned from rugby because of his illegal use of his elbow.

On my way down from Aberdare Crescent, I met Owen Williams, Minister of Carmel Congregational Church in Abergelly, a tall bespectacled individual whose figure was so lean that it must have been vulnerable to any stray gust of wind. His Manse was in the next street to the Vicarage. Its proximity had enabled me to play a prank on him a few weeks previously. I was weeding the drive clad in some old clothes and an open-necked shirt when a tramp appeared beside me as I knelt among the dandelions.

'Is the Vicar in?' he asked.

'I am afraid he is not,' I said. 'What do you want anyway?'

'Just a cup of tea and bite to eat,' he replied.

'If you go around the corner to 23 Penlan Avenue – that is the Manse – I am sure the Minister will provide you with a cup of tea and a sandwich or something.'

The next day I rang up the Minister. 'Did you have a

gentleman of the road asking for sustenance yesterday afternoon?' I enquired.

'I did indeed,' he said. 'Why do you ask?'

'I have to admit that I was responsible for his visit,' I replied. 'I was removing the weeds from my drive, a rare event, when he turned up. Since I was only just beginning my task, I thought perhaps that you would be better placed to deal with him.'

'Thank you indeed, Vicar,' he retorted. 'I shall make a point of directing all gentlemen of the road, as you call them, in your direction from now on. Be prepared for a hobo invasion.'

'Seen any tramps lately?' was his greeting.

'None, thank God,' I said. 'Evidently it must be the close season.'

'I am glad I have met you,' he went on. 'I should like your advice on something which I have had in mind for some time. I can't talk about it here but if you have a spare half hour, or maybe an hour, I should like to come across to the Vicarage and have a word with you.'

'By all means,' I replied. 'What about this evening? I have nothing on.'

'That's fine by me,' he said. 'If I come about seven o'clockish, will that be OK?'

'That will suit me nicely.'

So it was that at five past seven that evening, accompanied by Lulu, my faithful hound, I opened the door to the Reverend Owen Williams, BA, BD. Although he lived close by, our relationship was not much more than a nodding acquaintance. My telephone call about the tramp, prompted by my conscience, was the first time I had ventured beyond that stage. As I led him into my study, he said, 'Thank you, Vicar, for being so ready to give me some of your time.'

'Before you say any more,' I replied, 'shall we dispense with formality and address each other by our Christian names? I am Fred and you are Owen. I think that is the best way to begin our tête-à-tête. Before we talk, may I offer you some liquid refreshment? We have everything from tea and coffee to most of the alcoholic beverages.'

'Well, Fred,' he said, 'I would enjoy a glass of beer, if you have one.'

'In that case, I can offer you a bottle of the local brew,' I announced. Minutes later we shared the nectar of the nearest brewery. 'I wasn't quite sure whether you imbibed,' I told him.

'I am not a Baptist,' he replied, 'nor a Methodist if it comes to that. They are worse than the Baptists in that respect. To be quite honest, I expect most of my congregation would draw the line at a glass of beer. However, as someone who enjoyed a pint when he arrived home from the colliery, I can say that this is most welcome.'

'What job did you do at the colliery, Owen? I can't think of you as working at the surface with your height.'

He laughed at my reply. 'I can't even bend to tie up my shoes. No, I was up on top in the office as an accounts clerk, working from nine to five. I found it a chore. At school I had got six O levels, but my parents could not afford to keep me there. I went to night school and got three good A levels. Then I applied for a grant from the Council to enter the University at Cardiff backed by the Congregational Union. Having obtained my BA BD degrees, I had my first call at a chapel in the Rhondda. I was there only three years when I was invited to my present position at Abergelly. That was twelve years ago. This brings me to the reason for my visit this evening.'

'Before you go on,' I interjected, 'shall I top up your glass?'

'No more, thanks,' he said. 'I want to keep a clear head, if you don't mind.'

As I refilled my glass, he took a deep breath and launched into the reason for his visit. 'I am thinking of taking a different direction in my ministry. In other words, what are the prospects if I approached your Bishop with a request for ordination?'

Prompted by my surprised reaction, he went on. 'I can see that you are taken aback by this – er – declaration of intent. Let me explain. For some years now I have become increasingly disillusioned by my lack of authority in my church. The Deacons call the tune. Most of them are theologically illiterate but enjoy the power that their diaconate gives them. To say that they are parsimonious would be an understatement. Then again, I am weary of extempore prayer, prayer which is not really extempore but a series of clichés. I have a copy of the Book of Common Prayer at home and read it constantly these days. When I contrast the dignity and beauty of its language with the third-rate quality of what passes as a service every Sunday at Carmel, it makes me more determined than ever that I must do something about it. I think I have reached the point of no return. Now, I think you can top up my glass.'

There was a silence as I emptied the bottle into his shaky tumbler.

'First of all,' I said, 'as someone who has been brought up to love the Book of Common Prayer, I can only agree with your sentiments. On the subject of authority, it is true that the parish priest has considerably more authority than someone who is answerable to a body of laymen, so if you feel as strongly as you do about your present position, then there is only one course open to you. If you want me to pave the way for you by having a word with the Bishop, I shall be only too pleased to do so. I take it that you realize that for at least eighteen months or two years you will have to go to a theological college. I don't wish to pry into your private affairs, but how will you be able to cope with the financial implications involved in your transition from the Manse to the Vicarage? In other words, Owen, can you afford it?'

He smiled. 'Don't think that I have not considered that, Fred. My wife and I have no children. She was a school teacher before we married. Rhiannon is quite prepared to go back to teaching to become the breadwinner for a few years. In fact we shall have a bigger income as a result. Her one concern is that I shall be happy and fulfilled in what I am doing. At the moment she knows that I have been in the doldrums for some years. She is by no means a dedicated Congregationalist. Her childhood was spent in a Church in Wales school and her parents were twice a year worshippers at the parish church. She went to a church training college for teachers, so the Book of Common Prayer is nothing new to her.'

'In that case,' I replied, 'I shall ring the Bishop tomorrow morning and tell him that he will be receiving a letter from you. Before you write your epistle, I shall let you know what the episcopal reaction was to my call. I should think that he would be most sympathetic. He is a very understanding man of God.'

As Owen left the Vicarage he said, 'Not a word to anybody about our conversation.'

'As if I would,' I replied. We shook hands and I watched him walk up the drive with his head held high.

Eleanor appeared behind me. 'Well,' she murmured. 'What was that long chinwag all about?'

'You will never believe it,' I said.

'Try me,' she answered.

'Our friend Owen Williams wishes to abandon his congregation at Carmel and become an ordinand in the Church in Wales.'

'From what I know of the people who frequent Carmel,' replied my wife, 'I can fully believe it. The wonder is that he has not become an atheist.'

'Come off it,' I retorted. 'They are not as bad as that.'

'You must have been meeting the exceptions,' she said. 'You should hear what Mr Price the butcher has to say about them, and he used to go there for years until he could not put up with them any longer. Well done, Owen Williams, that will be one in the eye for them.'

'Whatever you may think about the Carmel congregation,' I replied, 'please do not say anything about Owen Williams' decision. He has asked me not to tell anybody.'

'My dear,' she said acidly, 'I am a doctor and any information or anything said to me confidentially has the seal of the confessional on it.'

Next morning I phoned the Bishop. I gave him all the details about the conversation I had had with the minister.

'There is no need for him to write to me,' he said. 'Would you ask him to give me a ring at ten thirty tomorrow morning to arrange a meeting? From what you have told me, it would appear that this is not an impulsive reaction to the situation in his chapel, but a genuine desire to serve our Lord in the ministry of the Church in Wales. I see from the newspaper that your talent enterprise was very successful. Congratulations, Fred. I hope it will be the means of raising the spiritual level as well as the financial. By the way, it might be a good idea to send a press cutting to the Earl of Duffryn since he has promised to pay half the cost of the new church at Brynfelin. It will do no harm to keep him informed of your energetic campaign to raise the necessary money.'

The Earl whose family had provided the funds to build the parish church in the last century lived in Devon. I had made an adventurous journey to his castle in the course of which I had a car accident. It was all worth while to secure his pledge to contribute such a generous amount, even if I did incur a dislocated jaw in the process.

I decided to call at the Manse rather than telephone. Rhiannon Williams opened the door to me. She was a large lady. Eleanor used to refer to the couple as the Reverend and Mrs Jack Sprat. The Minister's wife had a rosy complexion and a ready smile. The smile was very evident as she greeted me.

'Come on in, Vicar,' she said. 'Owen will be pleased to see you, I am sure. He is out in the back garden watching his runner beans grow. I don't know whether he thinks he will make them grow faster by hypnotizing them, or what.

Would you like a cup of tea and a few Welsh cakes? I am just baking them now.'

'I can smell them cooling,' I replied, 'and they are having an effect on my taste buds already. I should love to have some, washed down with a cup of tea.'

She led me into the front room. 'Sit down, please,' she said, indicating a large armchair covered in a pretty patterned chintz. 'I'll dig him out now.'

The mantelpiece was decorated with a variety of photographs which featured the couple's wedding, Owen in academic dress and earlier individual pictures of them in what would appear to be their courting days. On the walls were Rhiannon's framed teacher's certificate, Owen's degree certificates and a group photograph of Owen flanked by his dictatorial deacons outside Carmel Chapel. It was more like a dentist's waiting room than a family home. I wondered whether the decor would change if and when they inhabited a Vicarage. My musings were ended by the appearance of Owen.

'What a pleasure to see you,' he said. 'Your first visit to our abode and, I hope, not the last.'

'I am sure it will not be the last,' I replied, 'especially since my conversation with the Bishop this morning. He says that he would like you to give him a ring at ten thirty tomorrow morning to fix a meeting. He thinks that you are a genuine candidate for holy orders in the Church in Wales. So there you are, boyo, it's full speed ahead for you.'

At that moment Rhiannon knocked at the door and entered with a tray of tea and Welsh cakes. 'You are looking very happy, Owen,' she said. 'The runner beans must have exceeded your expectations.'

'Blow the runner beans!' he exclaimed. 'Fred here has brought some wonderful news. The Bishop wants to see me and it looks as if he is prepared to accept me for ordination.'

'Thank God for that,' she said fervently. 'I am sick and tired of seeing you moping about. What's more, I shall be able to spend a few more years back in the classroom instead of being confined to the Manse and Carmel Chapel. Vicar, I'm sorry it's tea and Welsh cakes, it should be caviar and champagne.'

'I don't like either,' I replied. 'I would much prefer what is in front of me. I take it that you are more than pleased with the news.'

'Pleased!' she shouted the word. 'I can't tell you how relieved I am that he has ended years of unhappiness at being a square peg in a round hole. Once he has received word that he has been accepted for ordination, I shall be only too ready to say goodbye to Carmel. Not only that, the very day he gets that word I shall be writing to the Director of Education applying for a post. Do you know, Fred – by the way, I hope you don't mind me calling you by your Christian name?'

I shook my head. 'Not at all, Rhiannon,' I replied, 'especially since you will be one of us before long.'

'That is what I was going to say,' she went on. 'I have always wanted to be a Vicar's wife, to be in charge of the Mothers' Union instead of being on the Committee of the Sisterhood; to have some status in the parish instead of being just the Minister's appendage. All I can say is, thank you for what you have done for Owen. He won't need to look for consolation in his runner beans any longer.' She went to him and gave him a hug. His frail frame looked in danger of being snapped by the ferocity of the embrace.

When we had finished the tea and Welsh cakes, there was a ring on the front door bell. Rhiannon went to the door, her footsteps thudding down the corridor outside the door of the parlour. 'Good morning, Mr Stephens,' she said.

Owen looked at me somewhat apprehensively. Malachi Stephens, known as Mal to his friends, and indeed to the population of Abergelly, was the senior deacon at Carmel. His furnishing business was the one and only store in the town and was a flourishing enterprise. He had a reputation for meanness, which had affected his fellow deacons. Owen Williams was existing on a pittance. During the eight years he had been at the Chapel he had not received any rise in his stipend. Business may have been booming for Mal, but as senior deacon and treasurer he kept a tight rein on the finances at Carmel. None of his good fortune ever flowed into the pocket of the Minister. He was a small thin man with an unpleasant habit of miming hand-washing à la Uriah Heep. On the one occasion my wife and I had visited his establishment to buy a bed for Elspeth, we were only too pleased to complete the purchase as quickly as possible to escape any further display of his unctuousness.

The conversation on the doorstep was very brief. Rhiannon knocked on the door and entered full of smiles. 'I have saved you from a fate worse than death, Owen,' she announced. 'I told old Money Bags that you were engaged in some important matters and that you would not be able to see him until this evening. You should have seen his face! He said that he had another appointment this evening and could you come to the shop tomorrow afternoon some time.'

'I shall not be looking forward to that encounter,' replied her husband, who was now looking even more apprehensive than he was when he first heard Rhiannon address the deacon on the doorstep. 'I wouldn't mind so much if I was certain of being accepted for ordination, but, as they say, don't count your chickens until they are hatched. As for our friend Malachi, I am sure he must be smelling a rat and he will be very suspicious when I meet him tomorrow.'

'If you don't mind me putting my oar in, Owen,' I said, 'you will have spoken to the Bishop by then. I think when you have done that you will feel greatly reassured. Once you have met him he will give you his assurance that you will be welcomed with open arms into the Church in Wales. I would not worry too much about chickens and rats, if I were you.' He gave me a wry smile and Rhiannon, who was standing behind him, gave me a broad smile and raised her thumb in salute. She was convinced that he was home and dry.

Later that evening at the Vicarage when Eleanor and I were relaxing in the lounge, I told her what had happened at the Manse and what the Bishop had told me previously.

'It just shows the power that an odious man like Mal Stephens can exercise over an educated man of God,' she said. 'Poor old Owen will feel like a bird released from his cage once his lordship has spoken to him tomorrow morning. We must have them here for a meal when matters have been settled. I tell you what, it will be the talk of

Abergelly. Above all, it will be one in the eye for that dreadful creep Malachi.' I began to laugh. 'What's tickled you?' she asked.

'I was just thinking of a story I heard once. A preacher was in full flight in a sermon about the minor prophets. So completely carried away was he that he did not realize he had been in the pulpit for more than an hour. "And now," he announced to his comatose congregation, "we come last of all to Malachi – where shall we put Malachi?" A little man in the front pew arose from his seat and shouted up at the orator above him: "You can put him in my seat, he's welcome to it if he can take it." Exit little man.'

'Tell me, Fred,' commented my wife, 'why is it always a little man who is involved in your stories? I suspect that it is part of a David versus Goliath syndrome, especially since you are only five foot seven. Anyway, I like it, even if it does not double me up in uncontrollable laughter.'

'You are very gracious, my love,' I said.

The next morning after Matins I told Hugh Thomas about Owen's desire to change direction in his ministry. He did not appear to be very enthusiastic about the news.

'Come on, Hugh,' I said, 'out with it. Is there something I don't know?'

'Well, Vicar,' he replied, 'it may be just a rumour, you know what people are like. I have heard that he is rather fond of the opposite sex.'

'You must be joking, Hugh,' I said. 'A more unlikely roué it would be difficult to find – an unprepossessing bean-pole of a man who wears thick spectacles and has such a diffident manner. Where did you get this information?'

'As I told you, Vicar,' he went on, 'it may be completely untrue. When I was visiting in Brynfelin a few weeks ago, Mrs Alexander in Glamorgan Terrace told me that he visits a woman who lives at the top of her road and that every so often he comes to her house and stays for quite a long time. Then when he leaves, she comes to the gate to send him off and they wave to each other until he disappears.'

'That is hardly true justification for a slur on his character,' I replied. 'Have you heard anything else with which to support the evidence that he is a ladies' man?'

'Someone who works in the office with Janet told her that he will hold on to the hands of the female members of his congregation, the more nubile ones I mean, for far too long when he greets them, occasionally putting his arms around them.'

'Apart from that,' I said, 'you have no other basis for the accusation that he is rather fond of the opposite sex?'

My Curate showed signs of irritation. 'You asked me to explain my attitude to the news of the Minister's decision to swap horses,' he grunted, 'and I have done so. I have also said that it may be just a rumour.'

'All right, Hugh,' I said. 'Calm down! I am grateful to you for passing on the information. We shall have to wait and see what transpires after his meeting with the Bishop.'

When I returned to the Vicarage, Eleanor was just about to set off for her surgery at Brynfelin. I told her what Hugh Thomas had reported about Owen. 'I would not dismiss that piece of gossip too lightly if I were you. Remember how lightly you regarded Gareth Morgan,' she said. 'Think on, lad, as our old Yorkshire consultant used to say in my student days.'

7

The following Friday morning, when I returned from Matins, I found an important-looking letter among the usual brown business envelopes on the Vicarage doormat. I recognized the sender immediately. It was the Earl of Duffryn who had replied by return of post to my letter. On my way to the study I collided with my wife who was on her way to collect the mail.

'Anything exciting?' she asked.

'Apart from the four dull-looking ones addressed to you,' I replied, 'there is one quite impressive embossed cream envelope addressed to me. The crest on the back is that of the Earl of Duffryn.'

'Come on then,' she ordered, 'open it before I go to work.' We went into the study. I produced the paper-knife my mother had given me for my birthday and made a great show of attacking the envelope.

'Don't mess about,' said Eleanor, 'hurry up! Let's see what's in it.'

'My dear Vicar,' it began, 'Thank you for your interesting letter. I am so pleased to hear about the Herculean efforts you are making to raise money for the new church. Next Saturday week I am coming down to Chepstow for the handicap race which bears my name and to present the trophy to the winner. I will be staying with Lord Belmont up in Breconshire and I should like to come down to your morning service in Abergelly the next day, after which perhaps you would take me to see the prefabricated building on the Brynmelin Estate before I return to Breconshire.'

'Good old Bishop!' I shouted. 'If it hadn't been for you I would not have been honoured with a visit from our distinguished patron.'

'What's this "I" business?' said my wife. 'You mean WE should not have been honoured. It is the whole parish which will benefit from the Bishop's suggestion. I'm off now before your head grows any larger.'

I sat at my desk reading the letter over and over again, wondering what could be done to impress his noble lordship. My first thought was that I should consult Tom Beynon, people's warden, the man whose ear was to the ground. I knew that he was working the two till ten shift and that I would find him at home during the morning, probably at work in his garden. As soon as I opened the door of my car, Lulu bounded out of the kitchen and occupied the front seat.

'I'm sorry about that,' said Mrs Cooper. 'She only had to hear you going round to the car and she was off like a shot.'

'Don't worry,' I replied, 'she's no trouble at all. I wish all front seat passengers were as well behaved as she is. I would prefer her there any day to David or Elspeth, believe me.'

As I thought, Tom was in the garden when I called. Winnie, his wife, was in her pinafore and her curlers, obviously disconcerted by a visit from the Vicar. A shy, pleasant lady, she was content to be in her husband's shadow. 'Go on down, Vicar,' she said. 'He's out there with his snails at the moment.'

When I went along the garden path, I was confronted by the sight of my warden seated on a stool with a biro in his hand, apparently giving his autograph to a snail.

'What on earth are you doing, Tom?' I enquired.

'It's a long story, Vicar,' he replied. 'So here it is in a nutshell – or should I say in a snail's shell.' He began to laugh uproariously at his wit, while I looked on bemused by the scene in front of me. 'Will Evans next door has been throwing his snails over the wall into my garden. At least, I think he has been doing that. To find out if it's true I have decided to mark all the snails I can find with this red biro, so tomorrow morning I'll examine the garden and if I find any snails with a red biro mark on them, I'll know it's true. Then I'll take them round and show them to him. I'm looking forward to seeing his face when I show him the evidence.'

'Quite a clever idea,' I said. 'Now then, for something more important than a snail war: the Earl of Duffryn is coming to a service in St Mary's, Abergelly, on Sunday week and is going to inspect the church at Brynfelin afterwards.'

'Never, Vicar!' he exclaimed. 'What's brought that on?'

'The Bishop suggested that I write to him, telling him about the successful talent scheme,' I replied. 'I had a letter back by return of post. Apparently he is going to Chepstow on the Saturday for the races and will be staying with his friend Lord Belmont up at Breconshire over the weekend.'

'The first thing to do,' said the people's warden, 'is to organize a cleaning party at St Mary's. I'll do that. From what I hear, Dai Elbow is taking Gareth's place up at Brynfelin. He'll be only too pleased to get them cracking up there. How about getting the organist to put on an anthem? Then we must pass the word around that the VIP is coming. Mind, knowing Abergelly, that will be no trouble at all. Have you told Ivor yet?'

'No, Tom,' I replied. 'I thought I would come and see you first since I knew you were working the two till ten shift.' His pleasure at my order of priorities was evident. 'I shall be going down to the school straight from here. I may as well have a word with Graham Webb, our dear organist, after I have seen Ivor. It may be that he will think a week is no time to learn an anthem – we'll see. Before I go, would you mind turning up at three tomorrow afternoon? I have a gypsy wedding. I don't expect any of them can read; in fact, the bridegroom cannot write his own name. So when it comes to singing the hymns, it will be just me and the Verger, who can't sing in time anyway. So if you lend your baritone notes in the rendition of the hymns, it will be a great help, and especially with the responses apart from the music.'

'I'll look forward to it, Vicar,' he said enthusiastically. 'It must be the first gypsy wedding in St Mary's. What a week this is going to be! Gypsies tomorrow and an Earl next Sunday. What will happen next, I wonder!'

When I arrived at Abergelly Secondary Modern School, it was morning break time and the playground was a chaos of noise and movement. I threaded my way through the throng and went down the empty corridor to the headmaster's office. Elizabeth Williams, school secretary and contralto lead in our Gilbert and Sullivan Society, was at her desk in the ante-room. 'What a pleasant surprise,' she said. 'Don't tell me you have come to offer me a part in the next production! Only playing, Vicar, I'll let Mr Hodges know that you are here.' She went to the door of the inner sanctum and announced my presence.

'Come in,' shouted Ivor. He came to greet me and waved me into a chair by the desk. 'Would you care to join me in a coffee?' he asked.

'With pleasure,' I replied.

'You know the Vicar's preference by now, Mrs Williams,' he said to her. He adhered to protocol strictly on school premises. She was Elizabeth at rehearsals. As I made myself comfortable in the padded chair he went on. 'This must be a matter of urgent business, I take it.'

'It is indeed,' I replied. 'We are to be honoured by a visit from the Earl of Duffryn on Sunday week. As you know, he is a gentleman who is prominent in the world of horse racing and he is coming to Chepstow on the Saturday to be present at the handicap race which bears his name and is funded by his money. He is coming to St Mary's for the Sunday morning service and he wants to see the prefabricated building at Brynfelin afterwards.'

'What a bolt from the blue!' he exclaimed.

'Not exactly,' I replied. 'The Bishop suggested that I should write to him and tell him about the success of the talent scheme. I had a letter back by return of post. I've had a word with Tom and he is going to organize a cleaning party for next week. He was wondering if Graham could put on an anthem.'

'You had better ask him after you leave here,' said the headmaster. 'I think he has an off period after the break, so you will find him in the green room, as he calls it. He has gone all theatrical after *Pirates*.'

When I had finished my coffee, I called in to see him. He was reclining in an armchair, smoking a cigarette and reading a book. 'Don't tell me that the gypsies have cancelled tomorrow's wedding. I have been looking forward to that. It will be something different,' he commented.

'Not at all,' I replied. 'You can look forward to something different on Sunday week as well. The Earl of Duffryn is attending our Family Communion.' He shot up in his seat. 'I was wondering whether you could get the choir to sing an anthem for the occasion,' I went on.

'I could get the choir to sing an anthem,' he replied. 'Whether it would be worthy of the occasion is a different matter. They have started to learn 'Jesu, Joy of Man's Desiring' but that's all it is, a start. I suppose if we can have three practices in the next week, we might be able to do a good job if it. I'll have a word with them on Sunday morning. The Earl of Duffryn. What do you know! He's the man who is going to pay half the cost of St David's when it is built, isn't he?'

'That's the man,' I said. 'So let's hope we can make a good impression.'

'I'll do my best,' replied the organist.

Saturday morning dawned bright and clear. The wireless weather forecast was optimistic. It looked as if the three o'clock wedding was going to be blessed with fine weather – which was just as well since the post-nuptial festivities were to be held in the open air on Abergelly

Common. Eleanor and the children had been invited to come with me. David and Elspeth woke in a state of high excitement. Mrs Cooper spent most of the morning trying to cope with them, while my wife was out on her visits. I was in my study trying to prepare my sermons for the next day. It became impossible for me to concentrate. The children were running up and down stairs, shouting and arguing. In the end I could stand it no longer. I flung open the door and shouted, 'QUIET!' using enough decibels to drown the voice of a town crier. There was an instant hush. 'One more lot of noise from you two,' I said, 'and there will be no afternoon with the gypsies for you.' Whether it was the shout or the threat, it was sufficient to ensure peace for the rest of the morning.

Then at twelve o'clock the phone rang as I was about to consult my biblical commentary on the third chapter of St Paul's letter to the Ephesians, which was the second lesson at Evensong. My heart sank as the unmistakable tones of the Rural Dean bade me good morning. 'Between you and me and the door post, as they say, I hear that the Earl of Duffryn is coming to your church a week tomorrow.' My heart sank further. 'I was wondering whether you would like me to come and help, shall I say. I know that your Curate will be up at Brynfelin for the service there, as it were. I thought perhaps that you would be glad to have someone to – er – reduce your shorthandedness on such a conspicuous occasion.'

I sent up an arrow prayer. 'That is very kind of you, Mr Rural Dean,' I said, 'but won't you be holding a service in your church at the same time?'

'It's the fourth Sunday in the month,' came the reply,

'and since it is Matins the lay reader can take the service, shall I say.'

I took a great leap of faith, relying on my arrow prayer. 'You see, I think the Bishop may be present since it was he who told me to contact the Earl. If that is so, then there will be no need of assistance.'

There was a silence at the other end. I could imagine him thinking what the Bishop would say if he found him there instead of at his own church. 'Ah well,' he replied, 'I had better stay here, then. There would be an awful lot of clogginess in the sanctuary, if I may put it that way. Would you – er – give my salutationness to him? I met him many years ago when he came as a boy with his father to the unveiling, as it were, of the head of his grandfather in Abergelly Town Hall. I don't think he will remember me.'

As I put the phone down, I felt impelled to get in touch with the Bishop, if only to salve my conscience. I should have let him know in any case of the result of my letter.

It was the Bishop's secretary who answered my call. 'I am not quite sure that he is in,' she said. 'If you wait a moment I shall go and check.' She came back breathless a minute or so later. 'You are lucky, Vicar. He was just about to drive off. Here he is.'

'Hallo, Fred,' came the somewhat irked voice. 'What can I do for you?'

'My apologies for troubling you, my lord,' I said, 'but I have had a letter from the Earl of Duffryn and he is coming to our service at St Mary's a week tomorrow and afterwards he will visit our church at Brynfelin. I wondered whether you would be free and whether you would care to come.'

'Splendid!' replied his lordship. 'I can't stop now to consult my diary but I will ring you about nine o'clock this evening and let you know.' My arrow prayer had worked.

When Eleanor came home to lunch, she said, 'You are looking very pleased with yourself.'

'It has been a strange morning,' I replied. 'First of all I had to contend with two extremely over-excited children, and after that with an over-ambitious Rural Dean who wanted to be present at the Earl of Duffryn's worship at St Mary's next week! However, the sum total is that it is quite likely that the Bishop will be with us at the service and the Rural Dean will not.'

'Secombe,' she said, 'you have the luck of the devil – sorry, I must rephrase that – the Lord is gracious unto you, O saintly one.'

'Enough of the "saintly",' I replied. 'I had to tell a fib to prevent the Rural Dean's appearance at our service. I told his reverence that the Bishop might be coming. As a result I had to phone his lordship to ask him if he would like to be present. He is ringing me tonight at nine. What is more, he sounds enthusiastic.'

'What a devious man you are,' she said.

Lunchtime was pandemonium. The children were too excited to eat and spent their time asking questions. 'Will they bring all their caravans? Can I have a ride on one of their horses? Will they do gypsy dances on the Common? Will they have a big fire and cook an ox on it?' At half past two I went across to the church. Eleanor had to do her weekend shopping and had taken the children with her to save Mrs Cooper any further aggravation. There was not a soul in sight as I opened up the church. I checked the registers after I had opened them on the vestry desk. The occupation of the father was given to me as 'horse dealer' and that of the bridegroom as 'scrap dealer'. The bride's occupation was left blank. Suddenly I heard an explosion of noise outside the open church door. I went down the aisle and discovered such a spectacle of colour that I shall never forget it. The ladies, young and old, in a variety of brightly hued dresses, were decorating the church paths. In another group were the men, in black waistcoats and trousers with red scarves knotted around their open-necked spotlessly clean white shirts. There was no sign of a caravan. They must have walked down from the Common, which was not very far away in any case. I could imagine the impact this gypsy invasion of Abergelly must have made on its inhabitants. Tom Beynon and Graham Webb made their way through the throng, wide-eyed at the sight which greeted them.

'I tell you what, Vicar' said Tom Beynon, 'I bet this is the prettiest wedding you will have this year, and for many more, I shouldn't wonder. All these lovely scarves around their heads and those beautiful dresses. Much better than when all those old gels come done up to the nines with those awful hats they've paid a lot of money for.'

'My thoughts exactly,' added Graham.

By now we had been joined by Joe the Verger who had come in through the side door. 'I've lit the candles, Vicar,' he said, 'and I've put the hymn books and prayer books out in the front pews ready for the bride and groom and their families.'

'I don't think they will need them, Joe, because I expect they can't read. Anyway I expect they will take them up in their hands and pretend to read.'

None of the congregation came into the church until the bride arrived in the front seat of a caravan, accompanied by her father and what I presumed to be her matron of honour. The bride was dressed in a delightful cream costume with bridal veil and carried a bouquet of pink carnations. Her arrival was greeted with fervent handclapping and shouts of salutation. There was no confetti but no bride could ever have had a warmer welcome. Then in a trice, the concourse disappeared into St Mary's, and with it every vestige of noise. As I waited at the door to greet the bride, behind me was a silence which could have betokened an empty church.

Bridget Palmer was a picture of virginal innocence, her swarthy skin and her deep brown eyes framed in a madonna-like headdress. Her nervous father and her female companion stood on either side of her. I had already told the bridegroom and his best man where to stand when the organ began to play the Wedding March. All the men in the church were seated together on the bridegroom's side and all the women on the bride's side.

'Will you all please stand,' I announced from the back of the church. The organist launched into the Wedding March. As he did so the bride turned to me.

'Where does my best woman stand?'

'Just behind you,' I replied. 'When you reach the front, pass your bouquet back to her.'

By the time we reached the bridegroom, he was in a state of great perturbation, relying on the arm of his best man to support him. After giving her bouquet to her best woman, Bridget turned to him and put her hand on his, holding tight. I announced the first hymn, 'Praise, my soul, the King of Heaven', after giving its number twice. There followed a duet between me and Tom Beynon.

As I turned to the couple and began the wedding service, the congregation listened intently. When it came to the vows I said, 'Joseph, wilt thou have this woman to thy wedded wife, to live together after God's ordinance in the holy estate of matrimony? Wilt thou love her, comfort her, honour and keep her in sickness and in health and, forsaking all others, keep thee only unto her, so long as ye both shall live?'

He looked at me in a daze and then nodded.

I whispered to him, 'Say, "I will."' He appeared to be deaf. 'Say, "I will",' I repeated loudly.

'I will,' he murmured. I decided not to press the matter and turned to Bridget, who provided a firm 'I will.'

'Who giveth this woman to be married to this man?' Her father came forward with a loud "I do, Parson.' There followed a confusion of hand-taking and hand-holding. Mr Palmer was loath to release his daughter's hand and the bridegroom was equally loath to accept it. Once the situation was resolved I had to face the task of leading Joseph through the marriage vows. Very slowly I began to spell out the words of the Book of Common Prayer. The first part of the vow was negotiated successfully. Then came 'according to God's holy ordinance'. He was like a horse in a show-jumping competition who refuses to attempt a high fence. I waited for a response but none was forthcoming. I decided to take him through it one word at a time.

'According,' I said, looking at him as if I were a hypnotist. He managed to say the word and the next ones until he reached 'ordinance'.

'Ordinance,' I repeated, emphasizing each syllable. Since there were only three syllables I felt sure that this would be sufficient. I was wrong.

'Say after me,' I said, after waiting for what seemed like an eternity, 'ord.'

'Ord,' he managed to utter.

'In.'

'In.'

'Ance.'

'Ance.'

The last part of the vow was 'and thereto I plight thee my troth'. I decided to follow the same syllabled approach. It worked, thank God. Bridget sailed through her test with flying colours.

When I asked for the ring to be placed on the prayer book, the best man turned to the best woman, who produced it from a purse which was secreted upon her person. The groom attempted to place it on the wrong finger, but was quickly taken in hand by the bride who pulled the ring off, gave it to him and indicated the correct finger with a fierce whisper, 'Come on, Joe!' Her admonition had the desired effect. As he held the ring on her finger he repeated the final vow after me, with only one falter on 'worldly goods'.

They knelt in front of me and I announced to the congregation that they were now man and wife. I then blessed them with the beautiful prayer of benediction, which had been said over the heads of Queen Elizabeth and her consort some years previously.

We moved up to the altar rails to the accompaniment of Psalm 67 said by myself and Tom Beynon in alternate verses. I instructed Bridget and Joe to kneel once again, this time at the altar rails. 'Let us pray,' I said. The congregation all sat with their heads bowed. As I looked down the aisle there was this awesome spring sight of a mass of colour on one side of the aisle and the sombre black on the other side.

'Lord, have mercy upon us.'

'Christ, have mercy upon us,' answered Tom Beynon and Graham Webb.

'Lord, have mercy upon us,' I responded. 'Our Father,' I began. In what was one of the most moving moments in my experience, this inert assembly came to life with a fervent recitation of the Lord's Prayer. 'Lead us, Heavenly Father' was another duet, a complete anticlimax. As we went into the vestry I wondered why I had bothered to arrange the playing of the hymns. It would have been much more impressive to have left the Pater Noster occupying centre stage.

'Can I sit down?' mumbled the bridegroom as he found his way to my chair by the desk.

'By all means,' I said and stood beside him with a pen, pointing out the place in the register where he had to place his cross. Behind us there was much hugging and kissing and a torrent of sound after their silence in the nave. Mrs Palmer, the matriarch who had led the procession into the Mothers' Union meeting, embraced me after the signing of the register.

'You are a lovely man, Reverend,' she announced. 'I shall never forget you. May the luck of the Blessed One be always on your head Now then, make sure that you and your family come and join us on the Common later on.'

'Have no fear, we'll be there,' I said, inspired by the occasion to rhyme a reply.

When Graham Webb produced a joyful rendering of Mendelssohn's Wedding March to accompany the bride and groom on their way down the aisle, there was much shouting and even whistling to greet them as they left the vestry.

'Now that is what I call a wedding,' said Graham when he came down from the organ. 'I would not have missed that for all the money in the world. The splendid duets from you and Tom Beynon, the most inspiring recitation of the Lord's Prayer that I have ever heard, and complete silence during the service. Then bang, wallop, that tremendous acclamation for the bride and groom. There will never be another wedding like it in St Mary's, I'm positive.'

When I went back to the Vicarage I found my two children in a state of high excitement, which had even affected Lulu. Suddenly the sedate hound had become a playful puppy, leaping at me as I came through the door and then running round in circles attempting to find the tail she did not possess.

'Frederick!' exclaimed my wife. 'For heaven's sake, do something to calm them down before I lose my sanity.'

'The trip to the Common is off,' I shouted. There was a silence as complete as that in the church. Elspeth's lip began to quiver and David looked as if his lip would follow suit at any second. 'The gypsies have told me that they will only allow my children to come if they are well behaved. From what I can see since I have come in, that is impossible – so your mother and I will go and leave you with Auntie Cooper.'

David came up to me. 'Dad, I promise on cubs' honour that I will be – er – well behaved, and Elspeth, won't you?' She nodded her head vigorously.

I turned to Eleanor. 'Do you think they will keep that promise, Mother?' Her face was a picture of painfully suppressed hilarity. I never address her as 'Mother'. That combined with the intense earnestness of the children caused her to turn away to hide her amusement. She produced a handkerchief and blew her nose.

'You see what you have done,' she said. 'You've made Mummy cry. That's how bad you have been. Well, since you have made that promise, I am sure that you will be good children on the Common. Come here and give me a kiss.'

They hugged their mother and smothered her with kisses. Lulu looked on solemnly as if ashamed of her unexpected exuberance. Half an hour later we set off to the wedding reception.

It was a lovely late afternoon. As we left the last of the straggling houses which bordered Abergelly Common, we could see the encampment in the distance, a half-circle of caravans in the midst of which a camp fire burned brightly, sending up clouds of smoke into the saffron sky. Horses and ponies grazed nearby. I pulled in off the road and drove slowly over the grass towards the semi-circle. When we got out of the car, the matriarch came to greet us. Behind her was a hive of activity. A gypsy fiddler was seated on the steps of a caravan, playing dance music to which some of the couples were dancing. The smell of roast pig filled the air as its carcass crackled on the wood fire.

'Welcome, Reverend and Mrs Reverend,' said Mrs Palmer, 'and these are the two little ones I could hear when I came to your house.' She caught hold of their hands. 'Come and meet some of my grandchildren.'

Elspeth was reluctant but David was eager for the acquaintanceship, especially since one little boy was astride a pony. Five minutes later Elspeth had entered one of the caravans with a little Romany of her own age, while my son was patting the pony and chatting to the rider.

'Now that they have found friends, would you like to come and see my home?' We followed her up the steps and into an exotic interior, where burnished brass and silver decorated the shelves and brightly coloured curtains adorned the windows. The grandmother invited us to sit on an immaculately made bed while she went to a cupboard and produced a bottle of whisky and some glasses.

'Now then,' she said, 'will you join me in a toast to Bridget and Joe with a spot of Irish spirits? I know they're rather young but Bridget has got an old head on her shoulders. Joe is lucky to have her, but he's a good lad and he's no fly-by-night.' She half-filled the tumblers. 'Here's to them both and may they always live in green pastures.'

While we sipped at our drinks she emptied hers in one gulp. 'That's the way to drink a gypsy toast,' she explained. 'Now come on out with your glasses,' she went on, 'and I'll introduce you to members of the families.' By the time we had met them all and finished our drinks, our heads were spinning. We were only too pleased to sit on the steps of Mrs Palmer's caravan to feast on the pork and the vegetables which had been cooked on another fire.

As we sat there a young man in a black suit and a black trilby had approached us.

'I'm Evan Williams,' he said, 'and I am a sort of pastor to the Romany communities in South Wales. Sorry I missed the wedding. I have just come from a funeral outside Swansea. In the midst of death, we are in life, as it were. These are lovely people here, honest and hardworking, not like some of the tinkers and vagabonds who pretend to be gypsies these days. The Palmers are an old Romany family, well known throughout Wales. I am so glad you married them in your church. Not all Vicars are prepared to do that. I can tell you something. They may not be able to read or sing hymns, but they are a lot more like the children of God than some of those who go to church, if you don't mind me saying so.'

'I don't mind one little bit, Evan,' I replied. 'I shan't ever forget the wedding this afternoon. It was an object lesson in reverence for so many who come to my church chattering through the service, with the men smelling like a brewery and the women more interested in what others are wearing.'

When we returned to the Vicarage that night we were a very happy family. David had achieved one of his ambitions, to ride a pony. Elspeth had enjoyed playing with dolls in the company of Bridie, her new-found friend. Eleanor and I had discovered a new world far removed from the mundane life of Abergelly. Mrs Cooper came to meet the children as they came into the hall. They vied with each other in passing on information about their time with the gypsies. Halfway through their noisy chatter, the phone rang. I looked at my watch. It was half past eight.

'The Bishop is early,' I said to my wife.

Instead of the Bishop, an agitated woman's voice asked to speak to Dr Secombe. My wife hurried to the phone. I went back to the children and Mrs Cooper, who were now in the kitchen.

'Well,' said our housekeeper, 'they have had a lovely time, haven't they? Let's hope they won't have gone too far over the top to get to sleep – you know what children are like.'

My wife came into the kitchen with a request for my car keys. I saw her to the door.

'Jane Thomas, a twelve-year-old from Glamorgan Terrace, has terrific pains in her stomach, according to her mother. It sounds like appendicitis to me. See you later, love. It's back to reality, isn't it? Get the kids tucked up in bed and kiss them goodnight for me. You can have yours later.' With that she was gone.

At nine o'clock to the second, the Bishop telephoned me. 'I am afraid, Fred,' said his lordship, 'I shall not be able to join you for your service and to meet the Earl of Duffryn. I have a confirmation service in Llandulais. I am so sorry. I should have enjoyed being with you. Please give my apologies to the Earl and I hope that all goes well.'

I went upstairs and sat with two excited children until their eyelids began to droop. I kissed them goodnight and waited to take more time over the goodnight kiss for my wife, whenever that would be.

8

'I wanted to be a jockey, but my mother wouldn't let me,' said William James as he counted the money in the vestry the next morning. 'Who knows, I could have been riding the Earl's horses.'

'The only thing that could have made you a jockey,' retorted Tom Beynon, 'is your size. I doubt if you would know one end of a horse from the other and as for trying to control one, the animal would have been controlling you.'

Excitement was high in the parish church after the announcement that the Earl of Duffryn would attend morning service the following Sunday. There had been numerous volunteers to form a working party to clean the church on the Friday. The choir were busy rehearsing the anthem as little groups indulged in animated conversations in the aisles long after the service had ended.

'I think I shall ask Elizabeth Williams if she will come and augment the contraltos,' suggested Ivor Hodges, and then he added quickly, 'that is if Graham agrees.'

'I am sure he will,' I replied. That was followed by a suggestion from Tom Beynon that perhaps the Abergelly Male Voice Choir could be invited to sing one of their party pieces.

'Now hold on, Tom,' I said, 'the Earl is coming to our Family Communion service, not a musical extravaganza. I think the importation of Elizabeth will be enough.'

When I told Eleanor about the Duffryn fever which had gripped the congregation and the wardens, she replied, 'It's not just the congregation, my dear. We have had a call from Ed Jenkins, the indefatigable newshound from the local press. His neighbour, Betty Williams, one of your fans, had come hot-foot to inform him that we were to be visited by near-royalty. He wants to come and see you tomorrow morning.'

'What do you mean, "one of my fans"?' I said indignantly. 'She is no different from any other member of the congregation.'

'Oh yes she is,' contradicted my wife. 'She is young and attractive and I think she fancies you, but that is beside the point. Once again you are to have publicity in Abergelly. So make the most of it, Frederick.'

'Coming back to Betty Williams,' I went on, 'she is courting a school teacher who is a much admired centre three-quarter in the Abergelly Rugby team, five inches taller than I am and with a physique which puts me in the category of a weed in comparison.'

'Sorry, love,' she said, 'I seem to have touched a raw nerve. I promise I will not refer to any of your fans any more. From now on, there are only members of your congregation whatever their age, their appearance or their desirability. Allow me to add one footnote: I am quite flattered to know that my husband is regarded as attractive to the opposite sex!'

After a Sunday dinner which was as short of conversation

as it was overloaded with Mrs Cooper's platter of vegetables and bread and butter pudding, I retired to the study with a packet of antacid tablets and the *Observer*. I was halfway through the leading article when there was a ring of the door bell. When there was no sign of Mrs Cooper or Eleanor going to the door, I arose reluctantly from the comfort of my armchair to discover the identity of the thoughtless caller who was disturbing the Sunday afternoon peace at the Vicarage. To my astonishment it was a grim-faced Dai Elbow who was standing militantly on the step. Before I could speak, he growled, 'Can I come in Vic?' His attitude was so completely out of character that I could only stare and nod. He followed me into the study. By now I had recovered my power of speech.

'Sit down, Dai,' I said tentatively. 'What's the matter? You look upset.'

He launched himself into the chair opposite me like a boxer seating himself in between rounds. 'What's all this about the Earl of Duffryn coming to the parish church next Sunday for service and then popping up to St David's for a look around after? Why can't he come to us for the service? After all, 'e's going to pay 'alf the cost of a new church up there. I should 'ave thought 'e should 'ave met the people up there, not this lot down 'ere.'

'Now, hold on, Dai,' I replied. 'First of all, that is what the Earl wants to do. I did not suggest that he came here for the service. That is his own programme for the day and it would be very rude of me to try to alter it. Second, I am sure that he would want to meet all the people who worship at St David's and particularly you, as the churchwarden.'

There was an instant reaction to my words. His mouth dropped open. 'Oh!' he said. 'Sorry, Vic, I've got the wrong end of the stick. I was talking to the Curate this morning. I didn't know anything about the Earl coming until then and from the way 'e was talking, I thought it was you who was arranging things.'

'I think I had better have a word with Hugh Thomas,' I replied. 'He should have known better than to stir up things at St David's. The Earl is quite keen to see a new church being built on the site, I can tell you, and after all, it is the people down here, as you put it, who will have to raise the money to pay half the cost.'

He was quick to defend the Curate. 'No, 'e wasn't trying to stir things up, Vic, 'e's not like that, fair play – I must 'ave mistook wot 'e was saying. No, you're quite right, it is the people down 'ere that are working 'ard to get the money to pay for things. Well, I'd better be on my way and leave you to read your paper. I'll see you next Sunday, if not before.' He held out his hand and grasped mine in his big paw with an intensity which was supposed to indicate the sincerity of his apology – my fingers ached for hours afterwards. When I saw him to the door, he was about to shake hands for the second time, but I evaded the outstretched hand and put my arm around his shoulders.

'I'm glad you were prepared to stand up for St David's,' I assured him, 'but I am as proud of that church as you are. Never forget that.'

There was a broad smile on his face as he left, a different man from the unknown warrior who had confronted me earlier. As I watched him go down the drive, my thoughts turned to my Curate and the cause of my steadfast supporter's defection. I determined to have a confrontation with him at Evensong.

When I told my wife about the incident, she said, 'I suppose our dear Hugh could see himself as the pioneering priest-in-charge with his fiancée presiding at the organ, in a wilderness of council estate housing, remote from the town hall which had planted them there. However, you must admit, Fred, that this is the first time that the young man has shown any sign of disloyalty. Perhaps you ought to make the occasional visit to the Family Communion service up there to let him know that he is not the Vicar of St David's but just the Curate.'

'Maybe you are right, love,' I replied. 'Still, I think if I put my foot down firmly this evening that will be sufficient to keep him in his place.'

'I hope you are right,' she said, 'but you know the saying that power corrupts, even if, in his case, it is delegated power.'

'Well, let's wait and see what his reaction will be like,' was my reply.

There was an unusually large congregation at Evensong, when the regular worshippers were joined by others who had come to find out more about the next Sunday's distinguished visitor. When Hugh appeared in the vestry he was not his ebullient self. He spoke little and retreated behind the clergy vestry door to put on his cassock, surplice, scarf and hood for an unconscionably long time. As the choir joined us for the vestry prayer, he caught sight of Elizabeth Williams, who had come for the post-Evensong rehearsal of next Sunday's anthem.

'Don't tell me you have been converted to Anglicanism,'

he said in a feeble attempt at sarcasm. Before she could reply I intervened.

'Mrs Williams has kindly come to join the choir for a one-off occasion,' I fixed a hostile glare upon him. 'Now then, let us pray,' I went on and then decided on an extempore prayer instead of the accustomed collect, since he was due to preach. I thought I would call upon the Lord to remind him that the pulpit was not a platform for the pique he felt at the Earl's choice of the parish church for his Sunday worship.

'May the music we sing and the words we hear be to thy praise and glory, O Lord, for the sake of thy Son, Jesus Christ, Our Lord, Amen.'

When he ascended the pulpit steps with a look of deadly intent, it was obvious that my prayer to the Lord had fallen upon deaf ears, both in heavenly and earthly places.

'I take my text from the Gospel according to St John, the fourteenth chapter, part of the second verse. "In my Father's house are many mansions." In Abergelly there are two: there is the stone-built structure, well appointed for public worship down through the years, and the other house of God, a prefab, hardly in the category of a mansion, on a hill outside the town. On that hill we trust and pray a permanent building will stand on the site now occupied by what is little more than a shed. It is to that place, one would think, that the future benefactor would come to join the faithful few who are carrying the banner of Christ. Instead, next Sunday he will be here as part of a large congregation, most of whom will have come to see the Earl of Duffryn, rather than to honour the presence of him who has exalted the humble and meek.'

By now my blood pressure was nearing boiling point. I felt an overwhelming urge to ask him to come down from the pulpit. However, I know that if I did, such a request would only add to the conflagration he was creating. When Ed Jenkins came to see me in the morning, he would be writing his article under the headline 'Vicar removed Curate from pulpit.' For the next ten minutes I held my peace, as Hugh Thomas harangued his uneasy listeners. His biblical references ranged from Jesus driving out the money changers from the temple to the Sermon on the Mount. It was a rant, not an address. Then it ended with the anticlimax: 'I am sure we shall all be grateful to the Earl of Duffryn in the years to come.' Most people must have wondered why he had spent so much time denigrating the parishioners of Abergelly, as well as the Earl himself. He spent so much time on his knees during the last hymn that he only rose to his feet during the final verse. I hoped it was a prayer of contrition.

It was a vain hope. As soon as the vestry prayer had ended my Curate made a swift move to the cupboard to divest himself of his canonicals. Before he could disengage himself from his cassock, I caught hold of his arm.

'I want to see you in the Vicarage.'

His face went ashen. 'But – er – but I am going somewhere with Janet,' he stammered.

'That can wait. Bring her with you,' I demanded. 'She can talk to my wife while you and I have a chat. You are not leaving here until you explain yourself.'

'I only spoke my mind,' he said defiantly.

'In that case,' I rejoined, 'you must listen to me speak my mind. I'll see you in my study in ten minutes' time.'

In his anxiety to escape from the vestry he collided with Tom Beynon, who was carrying the alms dish, loaded with collection plates. As the churchwarden staggered back from the impact, the dish went up in the air and deposited the offerings in a clatter of coins and plates on the vestry floor.

'You need to rush out, young man,' exclaimed Tom, 'after that exhibition in the pulpit, but first of all, you had better help me pick up the collection.'

Hugh Thomas was on his knees once again for quite a while as he strove frantically to gather the coins. Eventually the alms dish was refilled and the Curate made a shamefaced exit, looking somewhat dishevelled as he went to meet his fiancée.

'Well, Vicar,' said Tom Beynon, 'I have been in this church all my life, but I have never heard anything so insulting as what we heard this evening.'

'Don't worry, Tom,' I replied, 'he is coming to the Vicarage in a few minutes and he will remember what I have to say to him for the rest of his ministry. As Eleanor said this afternoon, he is beginning to think of himself as Vicar of St David's. When he leaves my study later on tonight, I can tell you that if he dares to give a repeat performance, he will be out of Abergelly and possibly out of the diocese as well. The Bishop will not tolerate such conduct from a young man who has only been ordained a few years. He is a talented and gifted priest. It will be a pity if his ego destroys him.'

A quarter of an hour later in my study Hugh Thomas was seated in an armchair, while I occupied the chair behind my desk. Janet was in the sitting room with

Eleanor, who was extremely irate about her fiancée's outburst.

'Now then, Hugh,' I began. 'What on earth has got into you? The Earl of Duffryn is coming to this parish next Sunday. The Bishop thinks that this is a significant move in the process of establishing a permanent church at Brynfelin. He has asked to come to our main morning service at the parish church and to meet some of our parishioners here, and then he wants to go to Brynfelin to see the place where a new church will be built and to meet those who will form the nucleus of the worshipping community, who will occupy it. I was confronted this afternoon by Dai Elbow, who has always been a loyal and hard-working supporter of all that I have been doing for St David's. He was given the impression by you that I had arranged the Earl's programme for next Sunday. I have never seen such an angry man upon my doorstep. He was mouthing all the nonsense that you were preaching from the pulpit this evening, obviously indoctrinated by your good self. Once he knew the truth that the Earl had fixed the details about his visit, he was profoundly apologetic. Not only that, but he was loyal to you, saying that he must have misunderstood what you had told him. If you had an ounce of that loyalty to me, you could not have made such a disgrace of yourself. I tell you this, Hugh, one more sermon like that and you will find yourself out of Abergelly, and if the Bishop knew of it, you would have to find another diocese, which would not be easy, I can tell you.'

During my tirade he kept his eyes fixed on his feet, his hands clasped firmly across his midriff so that his knuckles stood out white. When I finished, he took a deep breath and then raised his head with his eyes closed.

'I am afraid I got carried away, Vicar,' he said quietly. Then he opened his eyes and looked me full in the face. 'I am sorry. It is only now that I realize what I have done. St David's has come to mean so much to me, and not only the church, but the people of Brynfelin. I felt they were being short-changed and that I was going to make a stand on their behalf. Instead I have made a fool of myself, insulting you and the congregation at St Peter's. I give you my word that it will not happen again. I can't say any more than that and I hope you will forgive my rash outburst.'

There was a knock on the door at that moment. 'Come in,' I said. It was Mrs Cooper.

'Dr Secombe is having a cup of coffee with the Curate's young lady and she wants to know if you would like some in here.'

'Tell her we shall come and join them in the sitting room,' I replied. 'I take it that you would like a coffee, Hugh?'

There was a glimmer of a smile on his face. 'I'd love one,' he murmured. As she closed the door, he said, 'I take it that I am forgiven?'

'For this once, yes,' I replied, 'but if there's a next time, never.'

We stood up, shook hands and joined the ladies. 'So you have finished your business?' asked Eleanor.

'I think so,' I said. Janet moved on the settee to make room for her beloved to sit beside her. She was a greatly relieved 'young lady', who sat as close as she could to her beloved. By the time they left, hand in hand, harmony had been restored.

The next morning, Ed Jenkins appeared at the door in a Harold Wilson trench coat, notebook in hand. He was a little man with a beaky red nose, on which was balanced a pair of rimless spectacles and behind which a pair of squinting eyes peered at me.

'Good morning, Vicar,' he said in squeaky high-pitched tones. 'Is it convenient to have our interview?'

'By all means, Mr Jenkins,' I replied.

'Well, you know what it is like with you clergy,' he went on. 'You may get called away with a sudden death or some such.'

'There hasn't been a sudden death,' I said, 'so we had better get off the doorstep and come inside.'

Once inside the study and ensconced in the armchair, he leaned back and surveyed my bookshelves. 'You've got quite a library here, Vicar,' he commented. 'Not that you have much time to read them with all your busy life. It's more for reference than anything else, I suppose. Now then, down to business, as they say.' He spoke with the rapidity of a machine gun, running one sentence into another. 'All I know about the Earl is what I have read in the racing pages of the newspapers. Perhaps you could enlighten me about his connection with Abergelly and why he is prepared to pay half the cost of building a new church. We did a piece on your visit down to the Earl's home down in the South West somewhere, but I found very little information in it.'

'The reason for that, Mr Jenkins,' I replied, 'was that the young man who interviewed me was more interested in the car accident I had on my way down to Devon than he was in the purpose of my visit. However, let me reiterate what I told him. The Earl of Duffryn is a descendant of the coal owners whose family were responsible for the development of the industry in the middle years of the last century in this part of the world. They exploited the workers and salved their consciences by building churches where they could worship. The Earl's grandfather built the parish church here in Abergelly. When I discovered this, I wrote to the Earl to ask if he would assist with the building of a new church on the estate at Brynfelin. To my great delight he invited me to come and see him. To my even greater delight, he promised that he would pay half the cost of its erection, as long as the parish paid the other half. The council has given the temporary church a lease of ten years, after which it must be removed. So you see, it is a matter of urgency that the money must be found in a relatively short amount of time. So far, in a matter of twelve months or so, we have raised more than a thousand pounds towards our target. I informed the Earl of the success of the talent scheme which your paper reported. Since he is coming to Chepstow for the races on Saturday, he has said that he would like to join us for worship on Sunday morning at the parish church and then visit the temporary building at Brynfelin afterwards. There he will meet the faithful few who form the foundation of the new church which will arise towards the end of the 1960s. At the moment, as you know, this big estate has no shops, no school, no community centre of any kind. It is a concrete jungle. Perhaps the interest shown by the Earl will stir the council into doing something for the families they have deposited on the hill.'

It was quite obvious that Ed was an expert at short-hand, unlike the cub reporter who had endeavoured to record my words in longhand.

'Well, I must say, Vicar,' he said, 'you have a big under-taking on your hands. Evidently you expect no help in your task from the Abergelly Town Council, who have imposed a time limit on your plans and that's all. Moreover, you feel that they have neglected the families who live in the council houses they have erected. Thank you for your time. I shall give your words full prominence in my piece, I promise you. Will there be any chance of a brief interview with the Earl after the service?'

'I expect he will be in a hurry to get to Brynfelin,' I replied. 'Perhaps it would be better if you spoke to him up there, where he would have been able to see for himself the big task which faces the church.'

'I'll do that, Vicar,' he said, gave me a limp handshake and disappeared up the drive. I went back to my study and began to think out a sermon for the important occasion.

I had not been browsing through the biblical commen-tary for more than five minutes when the telephone rang. It was Will Evans, Vicar of Llanybedw, or 'Uncle Will' as he described himself to me.

'I'm coming down to Abergelly to do a bit of shopping. Will you mind if I drop in for a chat in an hour or so's time?'

'Not at all, Will,' I replied. 'Glad to see you.' A visit from him was always a tonic. There could not be a better start to the week.

I returned to my browsing only to hear the door bell ring for the second time that morning. I decided to let Mrs

Cooper answer the call. There was a short conversation, followed by a tap on the door. Our housekeeper's head appeared.

'It's that Scout officer, you know the one, a little man. He wants to have a word with you, very important, he says.'

I breathed a deep sigh. 'Show him in, Mrs Cooper.'

Willie James entered with a swagger which indicated trouble.

'Vicar!' he proclaimed in his ludicrously deep voice. 'Kind of you to see me. I hope I am not intruding.'

'Not at all,' I lied. 'Take a seat.'

His diminutive form was swallowed up by the armchair. 'I'll come straight to the point, Vicar. Would you like a guard of honour to greet our distinguished visitor next Sunday? Our troop was part of the guard of honour when the High Sheriff came to open the new Scouts headquarters a few months ago. Well, to be honest, it was just two of our best boys, but they were very good, I can tell you. So I thought if they could turn out for a High Sheriff, an Earl is much higher in rank than that. It will show how much the parish respects him. Well, there it is, in a nutshell.' He sat back and radiated self-importance from the depths of his armchair.

'The answer in a nutshell, Willie, is no!' I replied firmly. 'The Earl's visit is not a ceremonial occasion, it is a private visit. He is simply coming as one of the congregation to join in our Family Communion service. If it were the first Sunday in the month when the Scouts and Cubs have their parade, then it would make sense, but even then it would not warrant a guard of honour. I am sorry, Willie, I am afraid your kind suggestion is quite unacceptable.'

His reaction to my reply resembled that of someone who had received a dagger through his heart. He looked at me in disbelief that his offer of a bodyguard had been rejected. When he realized that nothing would persuade me to do otherwise, he stood up, all five foot of him, and then flounced out of my study with the words, 'Sorry, Vicar, I troubled you.' He went so quickly that I could not even see him off the premises. The front door closed with a bang.

It was a joy half an hour later to usher Will Evans into my study and to invite him to share a preprandial glass of beer.

'Well, boyo,' he boomed with a voice which could dominate any rurideaconal gathering, 'what's this I hear about the Earl of Duffryn visiting St Peter's next Sunday?'

'And where, may I ask, did you get that news from?' I enquired.

'Miss Theophilus, the organist at our church for the past forty years and very much a spinster of the parish, has a niece, Mrs May Wilson, who lives in Crumlin Road, Brynfelin. The Curate told her in church yesterday that the Earl was going to St Peter's for the parish Communion next Sunday and afterwards would be coming up to your prefab to meet the faithful few. What a turn up for the books, eh? How did you manage that?'

'To be honest,' I replied, 'it was the Bishop who was the catalyst.'

'You amaze me,' said Will. 'I know he is a splendid Father in God, but I have never thought of him as a catalyst.'

'To put it in a nutshell,' I went on, 'to quote someone who is a nutcase and who was sitting in your chair half an hour ago, his lordship suggested that I wrote to the Earl, informing him of the success of our talent enterprise. I had a reply by return of post. He said he would be at Chepstow for the races next Saturday and would come here the next day for our morning service at St Peter's, after which he would like to see our prefab, as you put it, and to meet the nucleus of a congregation. I have written to him giving the time of our service and thanking him for his interest.'

'So you should,' he replied. 'By the way, I must say your Curate is making quite an impact on the children who come to Sunday School up there.'

'What do you mean?' I asked.

'Well, a few Sundays ago, Mrs Wilson's children had come home from their service and were discussing what they had been taught. They were seated on the steps in the back garden drinking pop and eating chocolate biscuits. Their mother had the window down to the half in the kitchen as she was doing the washing up after their Sunday dinner. Through the opened window floated the conversation from her offspring. The eldest, aged eight, was saying, "God has made everything. He's made the earth and the flowers." "And he's made the sea and all the fishes," said the six-year-old, "and he has made all the animals that feed on the earth and the birds and the insects," added the eight-year-old. "And he has made all us people," went on the six-year-old. In the meanwhile, their four-year-old brother, who had been silent during this conversation, decided that the time had come for him to make his contribution. "But the Council made the houses," he said triumphantly.'

'What a graphic description, Will,' I commented. 'Anybody would think you had been an eye witness.'

'I must admit, I have embellished the story a little,' he replied. 'As a matter of fact, I used it in my sermon yesterday.'

'In that case,' I said, 'here's another story about the children in Brynfelin which you can use in a sermon. Hugh Thomas was on his way to St David's a few weeks ago, clad in his cassock. There were two little boys seated on the stone curb opposite the prefab, as you call it. The younger one, who was about four years old, asked him, "Are you the prime minister?" Before the Curate could reply, the older boy corrected him: "Don't be so daft, he's the minister, not the prime minister." Then he looked up at Hugh and said, "Eh, 'ow much to go in there?" pointing to the church. He thought it was some kind of cinema or amusement hall. Now I used that in a sermon a fortnight ago. What a challenge to anybody entering a church.'

'Fred, my boy,' said 'Uncle Will', 'I had better come down here now and then for some sermon material. Before I go, tell me, who was sitting in this chair earlier this morning, the gentleman who was a nutcase?'

'You know him quite well,' I replied. 'He is the Scout master who took our church Scouts to your parish and set fire to the forest behind your church. With a following wind it could have destroyed it, if you remember.'

'Can I ever forget him?' exclaimed Will. 'Tom Thumb with the droopy drawers and the jam jar glasses!'

'He came here to ask if the troop could form a guard of honour to greet the Earl,' I said. 'He was most hurt when I told him it was out of the question.'

'What a wise man you are, Frederick,' replied my friend. 'It would not have been the best introduction to St Peter's, Abergelly, if the noble gentleman had entered the porch with a Scout flag wrapped around his neck!'

9

'Here we go again!' Eleanor came in from her morning rounds, brandishing a copy of the midweek edition of the *Monmouthshire Gazette*. 'You wanted publicity about the Earl's generosity after your visit to his country home and all you had was a write up about your accident. This time it is publicity about your criticisms of Abergelly Town Council. I don't know why you bother.' She thrust the newspaper into my hand as I sat at my desk and stormed into the kitchen.

There in bold letters on the front page was the headline 'Vicar's Attack on Town Council'. Ed Jenkins had concentrated on my asides about the inadequacy of our local government, relegating the Earl of Duffryn to the position of an also ran. My first instinct was to pick up the telephone and complain to the editor. Then I had second thoughts. I realized that his reporter had recorded my criticism accurately. The people on Brynfelin would echo my sentiments wholeheartedly. He may have left the Earl's attendance at our service until the end of his piece of reporting, but the council tenants may not have read that if he had not drawn their attention to the front page article. If there had simply been a bald announcement that the aristocrat would be at the parish church for the Family Communion service, tucked away in the middle pages, the folk on the hill, as the Bishop once called them, would not have known anything about it.

Feeling assuaged by my second thoughts, I went into the kitchen for Mrs Cooper's corned beef and potato hash. 'Well?' demanded my wife as I took my seat at the table.

'It could have been worse,' I replied. She stared at me in disbelief. 'That headline on the front page,' I went on, 'will bring next Sunday to the notice of everybody at Brynfelin. I am only saying what they have been thinking ever since they were dumped there by the Council. Even if the noble lord's visit to the parish church merits one sentence, at least they know that he is coming and that the church cares about them. That sentence did mention that he was going to pay half the cost of a new building on the site.'

There was a silence, broken by our housekeeper's apology for the lack of any greens to accompany the hash. 'I'm sorry, Dr Secombe,' she said, 'I thought we had a tin of peas but when I looked I couldn't find any. I must have been under an apprehension.'

My wife looked at me and her stare had turned into an ill-concealed expression of mirth. She coughed and said, 'Not to worry, Mrs Cooper, I expect the children will have had greens with their school dinner. It is more important for them than it is for us. In any case, I am sure you will be able to get some fresh vegetables from Reg the Veg this afternoon, ready for dinner tonight.'

I had invited Hugh and Janet to join us for the evening meal to show that I bore no ill will towards him after his sermon at Evensong, with his subsequent retraction of his militancy. When I told Eleanor about the invitation to restore the 'entente cordiale', as I put it, she said, 'I am afraid that there will be nothing of the "cordiale" on my part. The more I think about his performance in the pulpit the less inclined I feel to trust him. If he can do that once, he can do it again. You are too soft, Frederick.'

That afternoon my wife was due to take her turn at the Abergelly Hospital Clinic. I decided to go with her and visit two members of the congregation who were recovering from operations. Frank Williams, a clerk at the Council Offices, had been treated for a hernia and Agnes Wilson, a seventy-year-old widow and grandmother, had been given a hip replacement. Frank was a sidesman and a regular at the parish church. A plump, jolly man in his fifties, he was sitting up reading the *Monmouthshire Gazette* when I came into the ward. His first words were, 'What do you mean attacking my bosses like this?' He pointed to the article on the front page and then held out his hand. He shook mine vigorously.

'Well done, Vicar!' he proclaimed. 'It's time somebody protested about their neglect of the Brynfelin Estate. Once they had put up the houses they thought they had done their job. I see enough of the Councillors to know that they couldn't care less about the people up there. Mind you, you'll have to expect some flak from the next council meeting. They will be falling over themselves to justify their policy of doing nothing. There's no money in the kitty to build a community centre or shopping centre and if they do something, it will mean putting up the rates and so on.'

He took off his glasses and indicated the chair beside the bed. 'That's enough of that,' he said with a beaming smile. 'Sit down, Vicar, and make yourself at home. How nice to see you.'

'That feeling is reciprocated, Frank,' I replied. 'I trust that your operation has been successful. I must say that you look in ridiculously good health for someone confined to a hospital bed.'

'Everything has gone like clockwork,' he said. 'Mr Rees Williams, the consultant who did the op, is a very good surgeon. By the way, he said he knew Dr Secombe quite well when I told him that you were my Vicar. He told me that if you were as good a Vicar as your wife was a doctor, then the parish could not be in better hands. That's what he said this morning when he came to have a look at me. What's more, he gave me the good news that if all goes well, I'll be home by Friday. I've been walking about around the ward, so with a bit a luck I'll be able to be in church for the big day next Sunday.'

'That's great, Frank,' I replied. 'We'll keep a seat for you near the front so that you won't have too far to walk to receive your Communion. I'll tell Tom Beynon when I see him on Friday.'

'Keep a seat for my missus as well, for heaven's sake,' he said, 'otherwise I'll never hear the end of it.' Eirys Williams was a female Neverwell, born to trouble as the sparks fly upward. As Frank told me once in a rare confidence, 'I have never known her to say that she feels well, even if she looks a picture of health. To be honest, Vicar, she's the embodiment of Mona Lott in Tommy Handley's *ITMA*.'

'Rest assured,' I informed him, 'there will be a place for your wife alongside you next Sunday.'

As soon as I entered the Prince of Wales Ward, Agnes Wilson began to wave frantically to attract my attention. I prepared myself for at least a half hour's incarceration at her bedside. Her wizened face had more lines than Clapham railway junction, as Eleanor once described it. It was surmounted by a sparse head of hair, dyed jet black. Her mouth contained an ill-fitting set of false teeth, which clicked like castanets with every consonant. Her speech was liberally sprinkled with the two words 'an' that'.

'How are you, Mrs Wilson?' I asked, knowing that I had no need of any further contribution to her subsequent monologue.

'Coming on, Vicar,' she began. 'Coming on. They say that it will take weeks before I can walk an' that and then only with a stick, an' that. Then it will be months before I can get about without a stick, an' that. So it's going to be a long job. I was down in the theatre for two hours having things done, an' that. The surgeon said that my hip was out of date, as it were, if you know what I mean. Anyway, he's put a pin job in there instead. So as long as I take it easy, an' that, I shan't have any more worries, an' that. Our Maureen says that she will see to everything in the house. She'll come over first thing in the morning once the children have gone to school and see to my breakfast, an' that, for the time being until I can do for myself. You can't ask anything more than that, can you, Vicar?'

I did not know whether to shake my head or nod. I just smiled at her. She seemed to think that my response was appropriate.

'Well, as I was saying,' she went on, 'it looks as if it won't be long before I get back to the Mothers' Union and to church, an' that. The Curate brought me Communion before I had my operation. He's lovely, isn't he? Janet is lucky to have him – mind, she's a good little girl. I've known her since she was a baby, an' that. How long before they'll get married, do you think, Vicar?' Before I could answer her question, she continued with her meanderings. 'I should think it will be quite a time with the cost of things, an' that. It's not like it was when I got married.'

To my great relief, a nurse appeared at the end of the bed. 'I'm afraid you will have to leave, Reverend. We have to give Mrs Wilson a blanket bath.'

I was out of the ward in a trice, eager to escape into the fresh air and the refuge of the car park. My head was ringing with the incessant chatter. The late Mr Wilson had died in his forties. It must have been a happy release. As I stood enjoying the silence, a car crawled to a halt alongside me. Smiling at me through the windscreen was the face of the Rural Dean. It was more an exhibition of his false teeth than a smile. He clambered out of the driving seat and closed the door carefully before locking it and trying the handle two or three times to ascertain that the vehicle was secure.

'Good afternoon, Vicar,' he said and shook my hand limply. 'Coming or going, as it were?'

'Going, Mr Rural Dean,' I replied.

'Well, before you go,' he said ominously, 'I wonder if you could – er – how shall I put it, fill up the breach for our Mothers' Union. They have their monthly get-togetherness tomorrow afternoon. Miss Atkinson was due to speak to them about her holiday in the Shetland Islands with magic lantern slides. She has just rung up before I came out to say that she has – er – what do you call it, you know, trouble with her throat.'

'Laryngitis?' I suggested.

'That's it, she could hardly speak. What with me having a problem with my hearingness and her problem with her whatever it is, it took me quite a while to know that she was not coming. Anyway, when I saw you now, I thought, this is the very man to step into her shoes, as it were. Perhaps you could give them your sermon from last Sunday.'

Since I had used the excuse of the Bishop's presumed appearance to turn down his self-invitation to take part in next Sunday's service, I felt that I had no alternative but to accede to his request. 'Right you are, Mr Rural Dean,' I replied, 'and what time is the meeting?'

'That is very kind of you, Vicar,' he said. 'The time is three o'clock, but if you can't get there by then, as it were, don't worry, because they never start on time. Mrs Bartlett-Evans is very punctualnessless. She has taken over from my wife as the one presiding over the Union members. Thank you very much for your Samaritanness.'

I walked back from the hospital knowing that I would have to wait at least another hour before my wife would finish her duties at the clinic. It was a pleasant late summer afternoon, ideal for a gentle amble back to the Vicarage. As I strolled down Wordsworth Avenue, one of the more prestigious roads in Abergelly, with its detached houses and well-kept front gardens, I mused about what I should speak on at the Rural Dean's Mothers' Union meeting the next day. My musings were interrupted by a loud voice exclaiming 'Vicar!' I stopped and looked around to find an elderly gentleman, holding a pair of garden shears, who was coming down his garden path towards me. He was dressed in an open-necked shirt, under a cardigan which had seen better days, and a pair of baggy trousers in the same condition. When he reached the garden gate, breathing heavily, he asked, 'Can you spare a few moments?' He was a little man whose sallow face did not indicate someone given to outdoor pursuits.

'By all means,' I replied. He opened the gate and shook my hand.

'Evan Jones,' he said, 'retired headmaster and Methodist once, now an atheist. Would you care to come in and have a cup of tea?'

'I'm very pleased to meet you, Mr Jones,' I told him. 'Yes, I would be glad of some refreshment after a stint of hospital visiting and of a chance of some intelligent conversation after listening to an old lady's empty gossip.'

'That does not come well from a man of the cloth,' he commented. 'I would have thought that the old lady, as you put it, would have been only too pleased to have someone like you to relieve the boredom of a stay in a hospital bed. My apologies, Vicar, for being so bold. However, come on in and have a cup of tea.'

I followed him into the hall, which was festooned with certificates of various kinds, and then into the sitting room with its expensive uncut moquette suite, where original watercolours of Welsh beauty spots adorned the walls. Evidently Evan Jones was enjoying his retirement. He beckoned me into an armchair and then disappeared into the kitchen. A few minutes later he returned, bearing a tray of tea and biscuits. 'You must excuse the rough and ready presentation,' he said, 'but my wife is at the Townswomen's Guild, one of her vices.'

Sitting in the comfort of the armchair and drinking Earl Grey from delicate china, I informed my host that I thought his 'rough and ready' presentation did not come into the category of a mug of tea minus tray.

'Many years ago, that would have been the case,' he replied. 'I began my working life underground, but fortune – I was going to say God – has been kind to me. This is why I have been moved, I think that is the word, to approach you. I was reading our local rag this morning and was disturbed to see the banner headline 'Vicar attacks Council'. You are evidently an honest young man who can see an injustice being perpetrated on the more feckless citizens of this community. I admire your candour, but let me warn you that you are sailing into uncharted waters. I know some of these Councillors. Under their sheep's clothing they are ravenous wolves, to quote the Sermon on the Mount, and, to mix my metaphors, I would suggest to you that a head-on confrontation with them will yield no fruit. Far better that you cultivate your friendship with them over the next few years. You have Alderman William Stewart living in your parish. Next year he will become Mayor of Abergelly. He will need a chaplain. As far as I know, the only place of spiritual refreshment for him is the whisky bottle. If you include him on your visiting list, that will achieve much more than a headline in the *Monmouthshire Gazette*. I hope you will not mind me telling you this. Believe me, it comes from the heart. I have known what it is to come out into the open and make known my convictions. It cost me a head-mastership I would have dearly loved to be mine. So, Vicar, if you want to see Brynfelin have its shops, its schools and all the other facilities essential to bind it into a community, please, please, accept my advice. Now then, would you like another cup of tea? I'm afraid I can't offer you anything stronger – you see, I still retain my Methodist abstention from strong liquor. I think that is the only relic of Methodism I have left in my life.'

'I am afraid I have to be on my way back to the Vicarage,' I replied, 'much as I would like to stay longer. Thank you for the tea and especially for your extremely helpful advice. Perhaps I might return for some more of your wisdom in the not too distant future.'

'By all means, Vicar,' he said. 'I am always available. Most of my time is spent in the garden or the armchair reading the latest library book. It has been a pleasure meeting you and may our next tête-à-tête be not too distant.'

When I arrived at the Vicarage, David and Elspeth had come home from school in the care of Mrs Cooper. They were engaged in a heated argument, watched by Lulu who sat like an impassive judge. Our housekeeper was preparing the greens from Reg the Veg, oblivious to the fracas behind her. It was a familiar domestic scene which I cherished as an antidote to the wear and tear of my parochial ministry.

Mrs Cooper turned from her culinary duties. 'Vicar, you've had a phone call from that Mr Stewart who's something on the Council. He said would you give him a ring. I've put the number on your reminder list.'

I went into the study humming the hymn 'God moves in a mysterious way'. I sat down at my desk and, with my hand shaking a little, dialled the Alderman's number. My call was answered by a lady whose tone altered when she heard that it was the Vicar at the other end. 'I'll get my husband for you now, Vicar.' Then I could hear her shouting, 'Bill, it's the Vicar.'

Moments later William Stewart's high-pitched nasal voice informed me that he had been reading the *Monmouthshire Gazette* that morning. 'I was surprised to find your remarks about the Town Council. Evidently you don't know the financial situation facing us.'

'Before you go any further, Alderman,' I said, 'I was about to ring you to arrange an appointment to discover the Council's intentions about the development of Brynfelin.' It was a white lie but near enough to the truth. I had taken Evan Jones' advice to heart and intended to approach William Stewart in the near rather than in the immediate future.

There was a pause while he sought to come to terms with the unexpected answer. 'Well, Vicar, let me see. Hold on a minute while I look at my diary.' It was more like five minutes than one before he returned to the phone. 'Sorry for the delay, Reverend. My wife had put the *Western Mail* on top of it. How about Tuesday of next week? How does the morning suit you, say about 11.30 a.m.?'

'Fine,' I replied. 'I have some sick Communions but they will be over by eleven o'clock.'

'Good,' he said. 'You say in the paper that the Earl of Duffryn will be coming to your 9.30 service. I suppose that anyone will be able to attend?'

'Of course,' I replied.

'Don't be surprised to see me there,' he said. 'The more support you get at the service the better, I'm sure you will agree.'

'Indeed,' I told him, 'especially when it comes from someone of standing in the community like yourself.'

As I put the phone down, leaving the Alderman preening his feathers, Eleanor returned from her clinic. She poked her head round the study door. 'What an afternoon!' she exclaimed. 'Half of Abergelly must have turned up at the hospital. How did your visiting go?'

'I have had a hectic afternoon too,' I said. 'I have been booked to star at the Rural Dean's Mothers' Union jamboree tomorrow, spent half an hour sipping Earl Grey in Wordsworth Avenue and, to crown it all, made my peace with the Mayor-Elect who will be at the service on Sunday.'

'Frederick,' she replied, 'you never cease to amaze me. Tell me more later.'

I sat at my desk and scribbled a few notes about the importance of family life in a Christian society. Since I would have an audience of grandmothers I realized that it would be advice on how to suck eggs, as far as they were concerned. I consoled myself with the thought that they would be looking forward to the tea and biscuits which would follow my few words, only too happy to have a talk which was short and sweet.

When I went into the kitchen David and Elspeth had their mouths too full of food to argue, much to the relief of my wife who was busy cutting up a large onion and shedding tears in the process. She wiped her eye with the back of her hand. 'Secombe,' she said, 'you really are hitting the high spots. Earl Grey in Wordsworth Avenue and the Earl of Duffryn in the parish church, not to mention the Mayor-Elect. Explain yourself, please.'

I reported in full the events of the afternoon.

'Just two comments,' came the reply. 'I should make use of that wise old owl in the Avenue if I were you and even more so of the Alderman. Perhaps an introduction to the Earl for that worthy gentleman would not be out of place. Now, if you will excuse me, I must make my contribution to the meal for this evening while Mrs Cooper is preparing the table.'

Hugh Thomas and his fiancée arrived outside the Vicarage in his MG, which was becoming increasingly noisy with the passage of time. They stood hand in hand on the doorstep. He was in mufti, sporting his college tie and wearing his jacket emblazoned with its cricketing emblem of the sporting elite at his university. Janet's hair was freshly permed and her summer dress appeared to be straight off the peg at Abergelly's Marks and Spencer. To quote Eleanor, they were 'love's young dream personified'.

It was not the kind of evening I had intended it to be. My wife was distant to my Curate but effusive to his fiancée. However, what did emerge from our conversation with Janet, who worked at the Council Offices, was the support I had from the clerical staff for my words in the local press and the antipathy of those Councillors whose remarks she had overheard that afternoon. When they went, Eleanor said, 'Praise God for William Stewart. At least you know now that you have a friend in court, and an influential one at that.'

The next afternoon I made my way to the Rural Dean's parish for my date with the ladies of Llansaint. Yesterday's sunshine had given place to that persistent drizzle which covers the hills and descends into the valleys. As the windscreen wipers removed the moisture with monotonous regularity, occasionally squeaking in a brief dry interval, I prayed silently for a day without rain on Sunday. Nothing could be more daunting to the visitor in this part of the world than when the clouds descend almost to ground level and create a sepulchral gloom, in which day becomes night. By the time I arrived at the small stone building which served as a church hall, the lights were on inside. Two old ladies approached me as I parked my car, their heads covered with rain hoods and their mackintoshes dripping.

'Good afternoon,' I said. 'Terrible day.'

They looked disappointed. 'Are you coming to speak to us today?'

'I am coming at short notice,' I told them.

'We were looking forward to the lady with the slides,' they replied.

'I am very sorry about that,' I said. 'I am afraid I haven't any slides. I have some holiday snaps at home but they would not be very interesting.'

I expected them to turn around and go back home. It seemed that they were made of sterner stuff. 'Ah, well,' said one of them, and they made their way into the hall as if they were about to enter a dentist's surgery. I had never felt less like speaking about the importance of family life in a Christian society. Suddenly it occurred to me that they would be far more interested in Gilbert and Sullivan and I wished I had brought a score of *The Pirates of Penzance* with me; but then on second thoughts I realized that most accompanists at Mothers' Union meetings found difficulty in playing hymn tunes. If I was going to sing, it would have to be unaccompanied. This became apparent when my entry into the hall was greeted by the uncertain notes of 'The King of Love my Shepherd is' emanating from the ancient upright piano, as an elderly lady was practising her contribution to the service. Half a dozen members were enjoying a gossip while a middle-aged lady in tweeds was thumbing through the pages of the Mothers' Union service book behind the table which faced two rows of wooden chairs.

When the presiding member became aware of my presence she came to greet me. Tall, thin, with a string of pearls decorating her expensive jumper, she was unlike any other in her position I had encountered. 'Ah, Vicar!' she said, in a tone of voice only to be heard in a country mansion. 'How kind of you to deputize at such short notice.' Then speaking *sotto voce* she went on, 'I'm glad we have been spared those boring photographs of Scotland that dear old Miss Atkinson trots out annually. If she went somewhere else at least it would be different.'

Emboldened by the attitude of this refreshingly different chairperson, I told her that I would be giving a talk on Gilbert and Sullivan. 'Wonderful!' she exclaimed. 'I am a fanatical Savoyard. Are you a performer, by any chance?'

'Indeed I am,' I replied. 'We have not long ago performed *Pirates*. I directed it and sang Frederic.'

'Why on earth did you not bring a score with you?' she demanded.

'To be honest,' I said, 'I had prepared a talk on Christian family life, but when I was informed by two ladies on my arrival that they had been looking forward to Miss Atkinson's slides, I thought that a sermon would be inappropriate under the circumstances, not to mention this dismal weather.'

'You are in luck, Vicar,' she announced. 'I know the score of *Pirates* very well, almost by heart. What did you sing?'

'Frederic,' I replied, 'but I know the Major-General's patter song too. It is one of my party pieces.'

'Well,' she said, 'what about Frederic's "Oh, is there not one maiden breast?", if you will pardon the indelicacy, and "I am the very model of a modern Major-General"?'

'Splendid,' I enthused, 'I shall give a general talk on the partnership between the two men and give the background to *Pirates*, finishing with the two songs.'

At that moment, the Rural Dean entered with his wife. He made a beeline for the two of us. 'Vicar,' he said, 'this is the Honourable Mrs Hamilton-Mackenzie, our – er – shall I say, foundation stone of the Mothers' Union.'

The 'foundation stone' looked at me with eyebrows raised. 'We have just been arranging the details of the concert we are putting on this afternoon,' she told him.

This time it was the Rural Dean's eyebrows which shot up. 'Concert?' he enquired.

'Mr Secombe is going to sing music from *The Pirates of Penzance*. I hope to provide some sort of accompaniment,' she said. 'I suppose you could call it tentative busking.'

'Well,' he remarked, 'you have bowled me over with a feather. Here I am expecting to hear, how shall I put it, some religious instructioness from our speaker. Instead he is doing a music hall piece of performing.'

'I think it will be a welcome change,' she retorted. 'In any case the members were expecting a film show of sorts from Miss Atkinson, not a sermon.' She banged on the table with a hymn book. 'Ladies!' she ordered. 'Will you please take your seats.'

The Reverend Llewellyn Evans and his wife took their places in the empty second row behind the front line of chairs, which was occupied by the eight members present. The honourable lady said the prayers and read the lesson in exemplary fashion, after the opening hymn in which the quality of the singing matched the excruciating rendition of the pianist.

'It gives me great pleasure to introduce the Vicar of Abergelly, the Reverend Fred Secombe,' she said. 'His subject is not a biblical one. It is the magical world of Gilbert and Sullivan, which has enthralled me ever since my childhood.' There were murmurs of approval from the audience. 'He will conclude his talk by singing two numbers from *The Pirates of Penzance*.' This time the murmurs were replaced by hand claps. 'I hope you will excuse the accompaniment, which I will provide from memory. In those immortal words, "Don't shoot the pianist, she's only doing her best." '

For a quarter of an hour I gave a potted history of the Savoy operas. Then I outlined the story of *Pirates* and moved to the piano, where I was joined by the volunteer accompanist. She played a few chords. 'I think I have the right key,' she whispered. 'I don't want you to develop a hernia. I'll just follow you quietly. You take centre stage.'

I launched into Frederic's appeal to the Major-General's daughters to rescue him from his slavery to pirate duty. For someone playing without a score and from memory, the Honourable Mrs Hamilton-Mackenzie was amazingly proficient. When it came to the second item, 'I am the very model of a modern Major-General', with its rapid-fire music, I marvelled at her virtuosity. The applause from the front row was unusually warm from a rural audience, echoed behind by Mrs Llewellyn Evans and watched by the Rural Dean, whose arms were folded.

As I left the hall to return to Abergelly, my morale was high. My pianist had praised my singing and my talk. There was an exciting weekend ahead of me. Sunday could not come quickly enough.

10

When Sunday did arrive it brought with it a cloudless sky and warm sunshine after days of rain. 'What a difference a day makes,' I sang as I looked out of the bedroom window. Eleanor was still in bed finishing her cup of tea.

'For heaven's sake, Frederick,' she complained. 'Keep your voice down. You will be waking the rest of the household. Save your vocal powers for the service this morning. In any case, you were off key!'

'I beg to differ,' I replied. 'Jealousy will get you nowhere. The great thing is that the Lord has given us a glorious day for the visit of his earlship. It will guarantee a full house. By the way, the choir were not off key at Friday night's practice. The anthem was spot on.'

'What do you expect,' she said, 'with so much G & S talent involved, from the musical director to the front ladies of the chorus? I think Graham should have chosen "Hail Poetry" as the set piece.'

'With all due deference,' I riposted, 'Gilbert's libretto on the poetic muse is hardly suitable for Family Communion. In any case, since it is sung unaccompanied, Graham would have been deprived of his virtuosity at the organ in "Jesu, Joy of Man's Desiring".'

'You win!' she said.

At nine o'clock when I went down to the parish church, worshippers were already filing into the porch. Some of them were unknown to me. When I went into the church, the four sidesmen were busy handing out hymn books and prayer books under the watchful eye of Tom Beynon.

'Vicar!' he proclaimed. 'By half past nine it will be standing room only.' The church bells began to peal out as he spoke. 'That's Ivor Hodges letting it rip,' he said. 'He's had them training on cornflakes all the week. I've put the reserved cards on all the front row of the left-hand side in case he comes with his friends from Brecon. By the way, his horse in the 2.30 came first, so he ought to be in a good mood.'

In the vestry Jimmy, my fourteen-year-old server, was in a state of great agitation. 'I can only find half a bottle of wine. That won't be enough to fill the chalice by the time they've all had a drink.'

'Don't worry, Jimmy,' I told him. 'If they receive their Communion respectfully, that will be enough. Anyway, there are two bottles of wine at the bottom of the clergy vestry cupboard.'

'In that case,' he said, 'I'll take the cruets out.'

As I made my way into the chancel, the scent of flowers was overpowering. The volunteer helpers had plundered their gardens, not to mention the local florist. In every nook and cranny there were vases indiscriminately crammed with blossom of various kinds. Abergelly was determined to show the noble lord that coal was not the only product of the valley. Graham Webb was sorting out his music on the organ stool prior to his onslaught on the instrument. The excited chatter in the nave was on its way to fever pitch. Sooner or later I would have to stand in the chancel and demand respect not only for the Earl of Duffryn but for the Almighty God in whose presence we had gathered. I looked at my wrist watch. It was ten past nine. I began to worry that my regular congregation would not be able to find a place in which to worship because of the plethora of publicity which attracted sightseers. My worry was exacerbated when Tom Beynon came up to me with the news that Alderman William Stewart had arrived with his wife plus his son and daughter-in-law.

'I've asked some people who have planted themselves in the front row opposite the places reserved for the Earl if they would mind moving back to the pew behind. I've never seen them before but they were quite shirty. Anyway, they have moved so I'll bring the Alderman and his family down. I thought perhaps you would want to meet them.'

'Thank you, Tom,' I said. 'This is becoming a circus instead of an act of worship. Once I have shown them into their seats, I think I had better read the riot act.'

I was surprised to find how short the civic dignitary was in height and how wide he was in cubic capacity. To Eleanor, he would be known as Humpty Dumpty, I felt sure. As he told me how much he was looking forward to the service and meeting the Earl afterwards, his breath indicated that his spiritual refreshment had begun already.

Once they were settled I stood on the chancel step and used my vocal powers, as Eleanor had suggested earlier, to request a modicum of silence. Competing with the noise from the belfry as well as that from the crowded nave, I shouted, 'This is God's house, not Abergelly Town Market. What kind of impression will the Earl of Duffryn take away with him if this behaviour continues?'

The effect of my appeal was an instant diminution of the uninhibited output of decibels which had prevailed until then. I went into my vestry and robed ready to greet our benefactor and his guests. As I made my way down the aisle, all conversation was muted, in sharp contrast to the pandemonium which had preceded my appeal for some restraint.

I stood outside in the sunshine at the lychgate and checked the time once again. The service was due to begin in little more than five minutes' time and there was still no sign of the Earl's arrival. As the minutes ticked by to 9.30, I became aware of the sweat on my forehead caused by my incessant pacing up and down combined with the effect of the sunshine, which was gathering in strength. Suddenly I heard hurried footsteps behind me. I turned around to see Mrs Cooper in evident distress.

'Vicar!' she gasped. 'It's the Earl. He's just phoned to say that his car has been held up by one of those jams after an accident. He was in a kiosk. He said he hoped he would be with you in a quarter of an hour but for you to carry on with your usual proceedings.'

She was accompanied by Lulu who had burst out of the Vicarage with her. The dog was about to jump at me when I snarled at her. 'Get back in that house!' As she went in the direction which I had pointed, our housekeeper apologized for the break-out.

'That's all right, Mrs Cooper,' I said. 'It's just the least of my worries.' I turned tail and went into the church where an anxious Tom Beynon was waiting.

'What was all that about, Vicar?'

'Apparently the noble lord has been held up by a traffic jam but he hopes to be here in a quarter of an hour. I don't know whether that is an act of faith or a realistic appraisal of the situation. The message he gave Mrs Cooper was that we should carry on with the service in any case. If only I knew where he was it would be some guide as to when we should expect him.'

'Well, Vicar,' he said, after due thought, 'I think we should wait until he comes. What about a warm-up with a few hymns?'

'Good idea, Tom,' I replied, 'but wait a minute – we are supposed to be celebrating the Holy Eucharist where our Lord is the central feature, not the Earl of Duffryn. I think it would be better if I asked Graham to play some organ music while we wait for him to arrive.'

'But Vicar,' he interjected, 'you know what it will be like. You won't hear Graham for the noise they will kick up while they are waiting.'

'Tom,' I said, 'you are a wise man. I think I shall go out and announce that we shall sing two appropriate hymns for the Eucharist. I'll have a few words with Graham first, of course.' As I made my way down the aisle against a background of noise more appropriate to the Plaza Cinema in Abergelly than its parish church, I thanked God for the wisdom he had bestowed upon the people's warden.

I went to the organ where Graham Webb was playing a Bach prelude. 'Let's have "Cwm Rhondda" and "Diadem". What with "Guide me O"' and "All hail the power of Jesu's name",' I suggested, 'that will occupy the congregation nicely until the star appears to top the bill.'

'Vicar!' he exploded. 'I never thought to hear such cynicism from your lips.'

'My dear Graham,' I replied, 'I am in extremis. What I thought to be a triumphant moment in the church history of Abergelly is turning out to be an anticlimax.'

'Whatever you say,' said the organist. 'I can only hope that the star arrives by the time we finish the two "rousers", otherwise the service is likely to degenerate into a session of community hymn-singing.'

I went to the chancel steps and announced that we would sing the two hymns as a prelude to the Holy Eucharist. I decided that I would say nothing about the delay in the Earl's arrival.

I went out into the sunshine, serenaded by the full-throated rendition of 'Cwm Rhondda'. It was the third verse of 'Diadem' which heralded the approach of the chauffeur-driven Rolls-Royce outside the lychgate. There was just the solitary figure of the Earl in the back of the limousine. The chauffeur alighted and opened the door for his employer.

On the last occasion I had met the Earl he had been clad in an open-necked shirt, pullover and baggy trousers. Now he was elegantly dressed in a grey suit, sporting a club tie which I could not identify; the only one I knew was the MCC specimen which I had remembered seeing on a cigarette card in my childhood. He came to greet me with his hand outstretched and a smile on his face. His tall figure towered over my five foot seven and a half.

'So sorry to be as late as this, Vicar,' he said. 'Had it not been for an interminable delay on the Heads of the Valley road, I should have been here in plenty of time. You shouldn't have waited for me, as I told the lady who answered the phone.'

'I had your message,' I replied, 'but I thought I would delay the service for a quarter of an hour. As it is everything has worked out well. The congregation are just coming to the end of the second hymn.'

'And very impressive it is, even from here,' he commented. I led him to the front pew where he knelt in splendid isolation. The choir followed me into the vestry from the chancel. As they did so, the girls began to comment on the handsome looks of our visitor.

'Shall we compose ourselves and think about the act of worship ahead of us?' I said sharply. 'Let us pray.' I intoned the vestry prayer slowly and deliberately to lower the excitement as much as I could. The first hymn on the service sheet was 'How sweet the name of Jesus sounds in a believer's ear' which came as a necessary calming influence on choir and congregation alike. Instead of the gradual hymn between the Epistle and the Gospel, the choir sang the set piece they had been rehearsing for the past ten days, 'Jesu, Joy of Man's Desiring'. It was a most moving performance.

When I went up into the pulpit to read the Gospel, which told the story of the ten lepers, I stood in complete silence. Not a cough was heard nor a rustle of sweet papers as they sat down to listen to my sermon.

'I told this story some weeks ago at a children's service in Brynfelin,' I began. 'I described the scene with the ten men shouting at Jesus to have mercy on them. What was wrong with those men that they wanted Jesus to put right? One boy put up his hand. "Deaf and dumb?" he said tentatively. The boy next to him dug him in the ribs. "Don't be so daft," he told him, "they was shouting!" There was a pause. Then another little boy put up his hand. "Gastro-enteritis?" he suggested.'

This brought quite a laugh from the congregation and the solitary occupant of the front pew.

'I tell you this story to illustrate the innocence and the ignorance of these children who are coming to church for the first time. Their knowledge of the Bible is not even minimal, it is zero, like that of their parents. There is a tremendous task in front of us to build a worshipping community on Brynfelin. To do this we must have a permanent house of God where that task can be centred. That is why we in the parish church have to strive to raise the money necessary to erect such a building. The success of the talent scheme is the first big step we have made towards that end. There will have to be many more before our goal is reached in ten years' time. What we must remember is that all our efforts would mean nothing without the extremely generous contribution which our esteemed visitor will make when we reach that target. We welcome him to St Peter's this morning and assure him that our gratitude will mirror that of the Samaritan leper in this story.'

From there I went on to emphasize that thanksgiving was an essential part of the Eucharist and of the Christian prayer life, ending with the prayer of St Richard of Chichester: 'Thanks be to thee, O Lord Jesus Christ.'

It was one of the most moving services I had ever taken. The reverence of the communicants was something I had not expected from the congregation's behaviour prior to the Earl's arrival. As soon as I had said the vestry prayer I went straight out into the nave to introduce our benefactor to the churchwardens. Ivor Hodges joined me after disrobing, while Tom Beynon threaded his way through the outgoing throng to get to the front pew where the Earl had remained after the service.

'Well, Vicar,' commented our visitor. 'That was a most rewarding Eucharist. The singing was inspired and your sermon very apt. Now these two gentlemen are your churchwardens, I presume?'

While he was talking to Tom and Ivor, I excused myself and went back to the vestry to disrobe ready for the visit to Brynfelin. By the time I returned, the three men were talking rugby.

'I hear your Curate was a promising outside half,' said the Earl.

'That was until he fell in love with the organist at Brynfelin,' I replied. 'He is now engaged and his thoughts no longer centre on the rugby field. You will meet them both shortly.'

'In any case,' he went on, 'from what you said in your sermon he will have his hands full coping with the housing estate on the hill.'

'You will be able to see for yourself in a few minutes what that entails,' I said.

'Speaking about our visit to your daughter church, or should I say your infant daughter church, would you mind travelling in my car to show Martin, my driver, the way? It will be a lot easier than trying to follow your car by the look of the numerous vehicles outside your gates. I promise that we shall bring you back down again.' With these words he began to make his way out of the pew.

Suddenly I became aware that Alderman William Stewart and his retinue were still in the pew opposite, obviously intent on an introduction. 'Before we leave, sir,' I said, 'may I introduce Alderman William Stewart, Mayor-Elect of Abergelly?'

'Pleased to meet you, your lordship,' proclaimed the civic dignitary in orotund tones. 'It is a great honour to have you in our borough, supporting our Vicar in his worthy campaign to give the people on Brynfelin a permanent place of worship.'

'Thank you for your kind words, Alderman,' replied the Earl. 'I can only hope that your Council will give full priority to the Vicar's aim of a permanent church on Brynfelin.' After they had shaken hands, followed by a similar gesture on the part of the Earl to the rest of the Stewart family, we emerged into the sunshine, watched by a crowd which outnumbered any wedding contingent at St Peter's. As I directed Martin, my fellow traveller in the back of the car began to comment on the anonymous concrete structures which lined our route. 'At least my forebears built homes made of stone,' he commented, 'but these have come out of a factory, not a quarry. I wonder how long they will last and how they will look after a decade of atmospheric pollution.'

Eventually we arrived at the patch of waste ground which houses St David's Church. There was a crowd of about fifty or so people standing outside. As we alighted from the Rolls-Royce, Hugh Thomas, clad in his cassock, came to meet us, accompanied by Dai Elbow.

'So you are the young man upon whose broad shoulders rests the responsibility for the pastoral care of this concrete wilderness,' said the noble lord. They shook hands.

'Welcome to Brynfelin, Sir,' replied my Curate. 'This is the churchwarden, Mr David Rees.'

'Great to see you, Earl,' was the greeting from the churchwarden. 'Glad to see your 'orse won yesterday, even if it was only by a neck.'

'So you are a sportsman, like your Curate,' said the Earl.

'Oh yes,' replied Dai. 'I played in the back row for Abergelly for years. Since then I train grey'ounds. As a matter of fact my bitch raised over a 'undred pounds for the talent scheme we've just 'ad.'

'Well done!' he exclaimed. Then, turning around to Hugh Thomas, he said, 'You must introduce me to your organist. I gather that she is your fiancée as well as your musical director, shall we say?' We moved down to those who were standing outside the church door.

'Where's Janet?' asked Hugh.

'She's gone back inside, Mr Thomas,' said Lily Evans, one of the Curate's youth group.

'In that case let's go inside,' suggested the Earl, 'where I can meet her and see what your temporary tabernacle looks like.' In we went, followed by the augmented congregation eager to hobnob with a member of the aristocracy. Janet was up at the harmonium, looking somewhat embarrassed. Her face went a deep crimson as the visitor shook her hand. 'I can see why you have given up rugby,' he said to Hugh.

'What about some music on this instrument while we look around the building?' he went on. The flustered young lady fumbled among the pile of music on the stool while we took a few steps down the aisle. I decided to let Hugh do all the talking.

'We have been given almost all the furniture by various churches,' explained the Curate. 'The benches, the chairs, even the altar. During the week we use the building for youth club activities and a women's group, and we are thinking of an old age pensioners' club.'

'Very laudable,' came the reply. By now Janet had begun to play Elgar's 'Chanson de Matin'. 'Now then,' said the Earl, 'you must introduce me to some more of your congregation.'

Hugh looked as embarrassed as Janet had been. It was quite obvious that for some of the crowd of onlookers, it was the first time that they had been inside the church. As Elgar's sugary tones came a little uncertainly from the harmonium, in front of him were three ladies whom he did not know. Fortunately for him the plumpest of the three announced herself as Mrs Iris Jones. 'These are my neighbours, Mrs Matthews and Mrs Hughes.' Behind them were four regular worshippers whom the Curate could identify. Eventually, when the Earl indicated that the time had come for him to return to Brecon, an overwrought Hugh Thomas was greatly relieved. As we stood outside on the waste ground looking down on Abergelly nestling below, the benefactor remarked, 'What a magnificent position for your church. It will be visible for miles around. All power to your elbow, young man, and indeed to your Vicar. After all, the financial donkey work will be yours. I look forward to the day when I come to the consecration of your new church. It is amazing how quickly the time will go for that great occasion to arrive.'

As we made our way down to the Vicarage, the Earl said to me, 'Do you realize I have not met your wife as yet? I must put that right before I get on my way. I seem to remember you telling me when we last met that she is a doctor.'

'She is indeed,' I replied, 'and what is more, her surgery is in a converted council house in Brynfelin. She chose to set up her practice there when she saw how deprived of amenities the inhabitants had been left by the Council.'

'How admirable,' he said. 'So you are both pioneering in that outpost of Abergelly. I look forward to meeting her.'

A few minutes later the Rolls-Royce entered the Vicarage drive. I fumbled in my pockets to find my keys only to recall that I had given them to Eleanor because she could not find hers. This meant that I should have no chance to forewarn her about the unexpected visitor. I waited for the Earl to leave the car. Together we stood on the doorstep as I rang the bell.

I had never seen my wife more nonplussed. The first to speak was the noble lord. 'Dr Secombe,' he said warmly, 'what a pleasure to meet you!' He extended his hand which she took somewhat timidly, unlike her usually forthright self. Then she recovered her composure.

'May I say that the pleasure is reciprocated. Please come on in.' As she ushered him into the sitting room, she gave me a hostile glance behind his back. 'Please take a seat,' she said. 'Would you care for a sherry or some other preprandial tipple?'

He smiled. 'Thank you for the kind offer,' he replied, 'but I must refuse. I have to be back in Brecon by lunchtime, so I am afraid that my visit must be extremely brief. I felt that I must come to meet you before I leave Abergelly. I enjoyed this morning's service very much and it was quite a delight to be with the people of Brynfelin afterwards. The only omission in my programme was an introduction to the lady who's not only the Vicar's wife but the physician who cares for her husband's parishioners' bodies as he does for their souls. That sounds quite poetical, doesn't it?' He stood up. 'Sorry to leave in such a hurry. Next time I come I shall take you up on the offer of a sherry. Thank you, Vicar, for an enjoyable and informative morning. I shall keep in touch with you and I shall be pleased if you do so with me.' We stood at the door and waved him off as the limousine moved silently away.

Once we were inside the Vicarage, Eleanor advanced upon me. 'Why on earth didn't you give me a warning, even if it was for a few seconds, that his highness had arrived?'

'I couldn't!' I replied. 'I did not have my keys on me, if you remember. I did think of doing a dash around the back door but that would have been very undignified. Anyway, I thought you coped with the surprise confrontation very well, very well indeed.' I gave her a peck on the cheek.

'Flattery, Secombe,' she said, 'will get you nowhere. More to the point, how did things go at Brynfelin?'

'Very well indeed,' I replied. 'I let Hugh do all the talking. There was quite a crowd there, most of them non-churchgoers who came out of curiosity. Poor Hugh had to introduce people he did not know. He was greatly relieved when the visit was over. Good old Dai Elbow was on top form, telling the Earl how pleased he was that his horse had come first and how his greyhound had raised a lot of money for the church. As his earlship said on our way back to the Vicarage, "You have a great character in your churchwarden up there, salt of the earth."'

'All in all, then,' said Eleanor, 'it sounds as if he is quite impressed by what he saw. Let us hope that the parish will respond to the visit with their sleeves rolled up, ready for stage two. Now then, my dear, Mrs Cooper has got her sleeves rolled up and Sunday dinner is just a quarter of an hour away, so what about a large preprandial sherry?'

When Hugh Thomas arrived in the vestry for Evensong, he was a different person from the one who sulked throughout the service on the previous Sunday.

'Thank you, Vicar,' he said, 'for allowing me to take over at St David's. It gave me great prestige among our small congregation. What's more, I feel sure that those who came out of curiosity will come again to worship one day. It may not be tomorrow, but the day will come. By the way, Ed Jenkins had a few words with the Earl when you were talking to Dai. He told me after you had gone that he was coming to the service this evening to "fill in some details", as he put it. So be prepared.'

'I am very glad to have that opportunity, Hugh,' I replied. 'This time I shall make sure that there will be no inflammatory headlines in the next edition of the *Monmouthshire Gazette*.

The choir were still 'on a high' as Ivor Hodges put it when he came to join them after his bellringing. I expected to see a small congregation after the morning's extravaganza. So it was a pleasant surprise to find an above average number as we came out of the vestry. There was no doubt that the Earl of Duffryn had provided a big fillip to my ministry in Abergelly.

The Curate excelled himself in his singing of the service. His intoning bordered on the operatic. Graham Webb at the organ competed with the excessive enthusiasm of the choir as they raced through the psalms, shaking his head as he pressed on the foot pedals, as if he was applying the brakes on a sports car. I was caught up by this euphoria when I ran up the steps of the pulpit, treading on my cassock in my haste to capitalize on the receptive atmosphere. The next moment I found myself face down on the worn out carpet. When I had detached my feet from my clerical clothing and hauled myself from the last but one of the steps, I found myself facing a congregation who were singing 'When in the slippery paths of youth with heedless steps I ran'.

My sense of humour fought a losing battle with my new-found evangelistic zeal. I decided to resort to my usual device to conceal my mirth by blowing my nose. My sermon was an anticlimax. As I strove to concentrate on my text, 'Behold, I make all things new,' I had to confront an audience some of whom were still giggling after five minutes. Remembering the advice I received in my student days to come down from the pulpit if no attention was paid to one's message, I came down after six minutes.

'I hope you didn't hurt yourself,' said Ivor Hodges, as I finished the vestry prayer.

'Only my pride,' I replied.

I was fully prepared for Ed Jenkins as he stood behind the congregation who were shaking hands with me as they left. When the last person, an elderly lady, had tottered up to me to say how much she had enjoyed the service, he advanced upon me with notebook at the ready. 'I hope you don't mind, Vicar,' he began, 'but I'd be grateful if you could fill me in with some details.'

'With pleasure, Mr Jenkins,' I replied. 'The one proviso I shall make is that there will be no lurid headline in your newspaper. I have had to endure two. I should be more than grateful if there is not a third.'

He blinked at me through his spectacles. 'That was the sub-editor,' he said. 'This time he will not be able to pick on the sensational in what you have said. It has been a most enjoyable day. All I want to know is something about the Earl's background.'

I supplied him with a full record of his ancestry and the importance of their role in the history of the valley. 'Thank you, Vicar,' he said. 'You may see me in church more often one of these days.'

'One of these days' never happened. More important was the headline in the midweek's edition: 'Earl praises church's work in Brynfelin'.

11

'I think the time has come to mention "planned giving" once again to the Parochial Church Council,' I said to Eleanor at breakfast on the Monday morning after the Earl's visit. 'There is such tremendous enthusiasm at the moment, so let's strike while the iron is hot.'

She looked up from her cornflakes and examined my face as if I were a patient. 'You really are on a high, aren't you, Secombe,' she replied. 'Before you get carried away by this tidal wave, I suggest you have a long talk with your wardens and especially with Tom Beynon. Ivor Hodges is more on the fringe of things but Tom knows this parish much better than you do. You couldn't have a better people's warden.'

Christian stewardship was a recent concept in church life in Britain. It was a transatlantic import and was being promoted by a professional organization with its headquarters in the USA. Any parish which decided that it would launch a campaign of 'planned giving' under its auspices would have to pay for the service of its expert who would stage-manage every stage of the campaign. It was not a decision which any parish could take lightly. On the other hand, I had heard of a widow from Canada who had settled in a nearby town and who put ten per cent of her income in the collection plate, despite having a family of five to rear. This I had described to my wife as 'heroic'. She called it 'feckless'.

Acting on her advice, as I almost invariably did, I called on Tom Beynon that morning before he began his afternoon shift. 'Come on in, Vicar,' he said heartily. That meant that his greeting could be heard halfway down the street. He took me into the front room. I could smell evidence of the Monday morning washing powder emanating from the back room as I came into the hall. 'Have a seat,' he invited. 'I don't suppose you would like a glass of stout this time of the morning?'

'No thanks, Tom,' I replied. 'What I would like would be a long talk about the next step of our efforts to get a church erected in Brynfelin.'

He sat down alongside me. 'Right you are, Vicar,' he said. 'Shoot, as they do say in the films.'

'I am wondering whether this is the moment when we should start a campaign of Christian stewardship in the parish. There is such a surge of enthusiasm in the congregation that I feel we should take advantage of it.'

'Excuse me, Vicar,' he said and disappeared from the room. I thought of the gypsy's warning from Eleanor. The next minute he was back with his pipe, his tobacco pouch and his box of Swan Vestas matches.

'Well, Vicar,' he began, stuffing his pipe with a liberal amount of Digger's Shag, 'I must say that we should think very carefully before we rush into anything that we could regret.' Then he struck a match and ignited the evil-smelling concoction. As he puffed out his first pipeful of smoke, he went on, 'It's one thing to ask people to raise money by getting others to pay for the fruit of their talents. It's quite another thing to get them to give out of their own pocket much more than they have been used to giving. This is not a wealthy parish, as you know. Apart from one or two like Ivor Hodges, all our congregation are working class, most of them paying rent for their houses and not having much left over at the end of the week to spend on any luxuries. What worries me is that some would be carried away on the spur of the moment to promise to give more than they could afford. In the end we'd lose not only their money but their attendance at church as well.'

By now the combination of clouds of his cheap tobacco smoke plus the force of his argument had diminished my ardour considerably. 'You must admit, Tom,' I protested feebly, 'that the amount of money in our weekly collections does not indicate even the slightest measure of self-sacrifice on the part of the congregation. Most of them give less than the price of a couple of pints and a packet of fish and chips or the price of the weekly rental of their TV set.'

'Maybe,' retorted the people's warden, 'but if you asked them what they would rather pay for – the rent of their TV or their church collection – I can tell you that the TV would come first. There's a new life beginning for them and you can't blame them if they want to enjoy it. I tell you what, I wouldn't be without our set. What did Macmillan say the other day? "You've never had it so good."' It was obvious that whatever plans I had to raise money for the new church, Tom Beynon would not favour a Christian stewardship campaign.

'Well then,' I said in desperation, 'what do you suggest we do to raise money?'

He blew out another cloud of smoke and looked at the ceiling. 'How about your brother?' he suggested. 'I tell you what, if he came to the Miners' Welfare we could charge what we like and we would have a sell out.' Harry and his fellow comedians Milligan and Sellers were now household names through *The Goon Show*, the most popular entertainment programme on radio. I was being pestered by clergy who were asking for his address, hoping that they could obtain his services to open their garden fêtes or bazaars. I had never imposed upon him before. So now, why should not his brother enlist his good offices to help in a good cause, I said to myself.

'I don't like using him in this way,' I replied, 'but I suppose he won't mind if I ask him to come to Abergelly as a one-off event.'

'I'll tell you what, Vicar,' said the churchwarden. 'The Earl of Duffryn may have caused a stir in the town, but your brother would make an even bigger one if he came. As far as the congregation's giving is concerned, I am sure that they will put more money in the collection plate than before when they see all the effort you are putting into raising money for the new church. Have a word with Ivor and see what he thinks.'

On my way back to the Vicarage an ancient Ford announced its presence by a loud blast on the horn. As it pulled up alongside me, Dai Elbow wound down its window. 'Can you spare a few minutes, Vic?' he enquired. I opened the door and just managed to get into the front seat before his back seat passenger attempted to make an escape. The next minute I was subjected to an assault on my person by his prize-winning greyhound, the chief contributor to the talent giving in the parish.

'Get down, dog,' yelled the driver. The animal slunk down behind me. 'She's only trying to be friendly,' I said.

'The trouble with 'er is that she's too friendly,' retorted her owner. 'Anyway, what I wanted to ask is if you would do me a great favour.'

'If I can possibly do so, I'll be only too pleased.' I replied.

'Well, it's like this, Vic,' he explained. 'My friend 'Arry Evans, the bookie, 'as 'ad a baby.'

'You mean his wife has had one,' I interrupted.

He laughed. 'Very funny, Vic,' he said. 'Well, 'e would like to 'ave 'er christened and 'e wondered if 'e could 'ave 'er done in St Peter's.'

'By all means,' I told him, 'but before that I would like to have a word with the parents. It is not something that you can order from a shop. It involves a commitment which you cannot take lightly.'

'I know that, Vic,' he replied. 'I said to 'im that our Vicar would 'ave to know a bit more before 'e could say yes.'

'Tell them that I can see them next Friday at half past seven.'

He sighed, 'I knew you would turn up trumps. Thanks, Vic.'

At lunch my wife indulged in one of her 'I told you so' responses when I informed her of Tom Beynon's advice and suggestion. 'I could see that a mile away,' she commented. 'You can't break a habit of giving to the church in an American-inspired commercial enterprise. Tom is much too old a hand to fall for such a short cut to some kind of ecclesiastical financial bonanza. As for the idea of inviting Harry to put on a show in the Miners' Welfare Hall, I think that is an inspired contribution to the brainwave schemes for fund raising. Now that is a winner.'

'Excuse me!' I said indignantly. 'I had thought of that before when I was being forever asked for his address and his telephone number by half the diocese. It is hardly a brilliant idea. Until now I felt it was not right that I should use my brother for my own advantage. Why should he step in to pay towards the cost of building a new church when the people who are supposed to be responsible are not prepared to give anything worth while out of their own pockets?'

'Now calm down, my dear,' she replied softly. 'Just look at things from Tom Beynon's point of view. You and I could contribute a fair-sized weekly sum to the church without impinging on our income. To almost all of your congregation, it would mean a sacrifice of their standard of living, if we can call it that, which would be quite disproportionate to that of our own. Do you realize what you are asking them to do?'

For the second time that day I had to admit defeat.

Later in the evening I rang my brother. 'Of course, Fred,' was his reply when I asked him if he would come to Abergelly. 'The only thing is that it will have to be when I am free. Tomorrow I'll call in at the office to find a date that's suitable. I'll tell you what, make it a Midnight Matinée. That's the latest thing. I'll bring my own pianist. How about an orchestra?'

'Well, we have one for our Gilbert and Sullivan do's. They are part-time professionals, if you can call them that, but they are quite good, I can promise you. Our church organist, who is the music master at our local school, is the MD. He's young, ambitious and very competent.'

'Fine,' he said. 'I'll send down the band parts in advance to give them a chance to rehearse.' After we had chatted about family matters, we both shouted 'UP!' and finished the phone call. I do not know why we did this, but we still sign off even today in the same way. It is one of those family idiosyncrasies which are some kind of bonding symbol.

Next morning after Matins, Hugh Thomas asked me what I intended to do next. 'I had thought of a Christian stewardship campaign,' I said, 'but after a consultation with Tom Beynon, I have decided to bring some more publicity to Abergelly by inviting my brother to do a Midnight Matinée in the Miners' Welfare Hall.'

I was surprised by the enthusiasm with which my announcement was greeted. 'Wonderful!' exclaimed my Curate. 'To be honest, I was a bit afraid that you would start a Christian stewardship campaign.'

'Why was that, Hugh?' I enquired.

'Well,' he said, 'I had a letter a week or so ago from someone who was in college with me. He is in the London diocese. Anyway, in it he said that his Vicar had turned to one of these professional organizations to raise the level of giving in the parish. The expert organizer swept into the scene, transformed the vestry into an office, installed a telephone line and demanded a list of church members with an estimated income opposite each name. Then began an assault on each one by a select band of amateur insurance agents, whose expertise was far below that of the organizer. Eventually, when the campaign ended, the net result was not a great leap in the bank by collections – what was more devastating was the telephone bill in the vestry. According to someone who had been friendly with the organizer, he had a special girlfriend who was in a ballet company in New York. I did not like to tell you this in case you would be influenced by a one-off incident.'

'My dear Hugh,' I replied, 'you could not have been more helpful. From now on our efforts will have to be concentrated on a varied programme of money raising and not on an all-out onslaught on the pockets of the congregation.'

As he promised, my brother rang me later in the morning with the date for his Midnight Matinée. 'It will be Thursday 29 November, so reserve a room for me in your ecclesiastical hotel, boyo!' he said. 'You've got all mod cons, I take it?'

'Of course, you idiot,' I replied. 'Vicarages are past the stage of cold-water basins and chamber pots. You will have a carpeted floor in your bedroom, not oil cloth, and the alternative of a shower or a bath in the bathroom.'

'Only playing,' he said. 'UP!'

After his phone call I went down to Abergelly Secondary Modern School just in time for the mid-morning break. I was greeted with enthusiasm by Ivor Hodges. 'What a great day last Sunday was! My apologies for ending a sentence ungrammatically, Vicar, but it was the kind of occasion which takes no account of the rules of grammar. So how do we follow that?'

'To be honest, Ivor,' I replied, 'I was thinking of a Christian stewardship campaign, but I have been persuaded by Tom, plus my wife, plus Hugh Thomas, that it would be a non-starter.'

'Well that's a formidable opposition front bench, I must say,' he commented.

'I shan't go into the reasons,' I went on, 'but instead I have decided to embark on a programme of money-raising events beginning with a Midnight Matinée at the Miners' Welfare on Thursday 29 November, featuring my brother. I was coming to ask you for your opinion about Christian stewardship, but in view of the concerted "no" I have met so far, I thought we should try something different. I hope you don't mind that I have gone ahead by asking my brother to put on a show without consulting my warden first.'

He laughed. 'Of course not. I think it is splendid that Harry has agreed to come to Abergelly. That will really set the town alight. On the other hand, I think that sooner or later we shall have to do something to raise the level of giving in the parish. I know that Tom has his finger on the pulse of the congregation, much more so than I. Money-raising events are fine in their way, but there comes a time when they will not work any more. That will be the signal for Christian stewardship to begin.'

'By the way,' I said, 'would you mind if I had a word with Graham Webb? My brother says he will need an orchestra and that he will send the band parts a week before to give time for rehearsal.'

Graham was enjoying himself playing a piece by Scarlatti when I found him in the school hall. He finished with a flourish of notes when he found me alongside him. 'Well, Vicar,' he enquired, 'what can I do for you?'

'How about recruiting an orchestra to accompany my brother in a Midnight Matinée at the Miners' Welfare Hall on Thursday 29 November?' I said. He arose from the piano stool and stared at me.

'Never!' he exclaimed.

'It is not never,' I replied, 'it is November the 29th. The band parts will arrive in Abergelly the week before to give you a chance to prepare for the big night.'

His normally impassive face broadened into a smile. 'Wonderful!' he exclaimed once again. 'I'll get together most of our G and S lot and augment them with a bigger brass section. I'll start phoning around tonight – what about a supporting bill?' he asked.

'I'm afraid I haven't got round to that yet,' I said. 'I'm sure the Abergelly Male Voice Choir will be only too pleased to appear, for a start. Perhaps I should ring Harry and find out what he needs as the rest of the programme.'

'If I were you, Vicar, I should do that as soon as possible,' he replied.

'In that case, Graham,' I said, 'I'll phone him tonight.'

By Friday, after consultation with my brother, the Midnight Matinée's supporting bill was complete, with the Abergelly Male Voice Choir, Elizabeth Williams (contralto), the four Rhythm Boys (a group from Pontypool), Joe Williams (an impressionist from Merthyr) and compère Frank Wilson, (a friend of Graham's) who was well known to listeners on Welsh radio. As Eleanor said, it was quite a respectable line-up.

At half past seven that evening, Mr and Mrs Harry Evans appeared on my doorstep, their expensive Jaguar gleaming as the porch light shone upon it. The bookmaker was a little man in his early thirties, prematurely bald, immaculately dressed in a dark grey worsted suit and sporting a club tie of some description. His wife, who appeared to be in her late teens, was clad in a short dress adorned with polka dots and with a sable coat around her shoulders. Her blonde hair cascaded over the fur coat.

'Ah! Mr and Mrs Evans,' I said. 'Please come on in.' They followed me into my study where I beckoned them to sit on the settee after I had shaken hands with them. They sat in silence as I returned to the chair behind my desk. 'I understand from Mr David Rees that you would like to have your baby christened in St Peter's,' I told them.

'Well, let's put all our cards on the table,' said the bookmaker. 'I know we don't come to church, Vicar, but I was brought up C of E. As a matter of fact, I was confirmed when I was eleven. I've got to admit that it is some years since I last took Communion. Shirley's parents are Baptist,' (she nodded) 'but they don't go to church any more,' (she nodded again) 'so perhaps, with the birth of our daughter,' (he gave her hand a squeeze) 'we can both make a fresh start, like.' Then they looked into each other's eyes.

I looked at them. 'That is the kind of thing I like to hear from parents who want to have their child baptized. There has to be a commitment on their part. In the service you and the godparents have to make a solemn promise that your daughter will be brought up in the Church's faith and that when she is old enough she will be confirmed. So many parents take this lightly. It is good to hear you say that you will not do so. By the way, what name or names have you given to your daughter?'

Shirley opened her mouth for the first time. 'Diana Dorothy,' she proclaimed with pride, her valleys accent singing the words. By now she had discarded the shy little girl act and was ready to add further details. 'Eight pounds seven ounces she was. She's put on three ounces in a week. I'm feeding her myself, aren't I, Harry?' It was his turn to nod. 'We've got a hundred and twenty invitations ready once you tell us the date, Vicar. Haven't we, Harry?' He nodded again. 'We're having the reception afterwards at the British Legion. Harry has ordered a beautiful cake from Cardiff. It's being made like a little baby.' She delved into the handbag she was carrying and produced a trade photograph of the expensive cake, with a cherubic face and a rounded body.

'I must say, I have never seen anything like that before,' I commented. 'Most impressive. Now then, shall we fix the Sunday? I hold baptisms on the first Sunday of the month. That rules out next Sunday. So it will have to be the first Sunday in November.'

'You don't do one-off ones, by any chance?' enquired the bookmaker. 'After all, you don't get many where a hundred and twenty people turn up for one christening. I'll make it worth your while.'

'I am afraid not,' I said very firmly. 'What is more, I shall expect to see you both in church for Family Communion at least once before the baptism.'

'That's all right, Harry,' Shirley assured him, 'I'll feed the baby earlier that Sunday.'

Her husband took her hand. 'Are you sure that's OK, love?'

'Of course I'm sure,' she snapped. 'If that is what the Vicar wants, and that is the only way we can get her done, then that's it, isn't it?'

'Yes, love,' he replied meekly. As I saw them off from the Vicarage doorstep with the Jaguar screeching its way through the gravel, I wondered what the odds would be against them making an appearance at Family Communion.

When I told Eleanor about the interview with Mr and Mrs Evans, I was surprised by her reaction. 'Why on earth didn't you accept the bookie's offer to make it worth while?' she said. 'The more money we can get towards the new church, the better.'

'My dear love,' I retorted, 'you are always claiming that I am a soft touch. Here I am making a stand against bribery and corruption and you say that I should have accepted money from a bookmaker to abandon the monthly administration of baptism.'

'Oh come off it!' she exclaimed. 'You would not be breaking some church law by holding a christening on some other Sunday than the first in the month. What about the baptism of David and Elspeth? They were "done", as our Shirley put it, by the Bishop on other Sundays of the month, so what's good for the goose is good for the gander.'

'That, Eleanor,' I retorted, 'was below the belt. How can you compare a sordid attempt to get special treatment from someone who has not set foot in a church for years? Surely we were entitled to have our children given the privilege of Holy Baptism by his lordship with all due ceremony by reason of my service to the Church?'

'Now calm down, Frederick,' she said. 'I apologize. That was below the belt. I know what a mountain you have to climb to pay for that church and I thought that any financial help you can get to that end is worth it. I am sorry I used our children's baptism as an argument to support Harry Evans.' She kissed me. 'I love you,' she murmured.

Our amorous interlude was interrupted by a telephone call. It was Ed Jenkins. 'I hear on the grapevine that your brother is going to do a Midnight Matinée at the Miners' Welfare,' he said. 'Do you mind if I come around to see you tomorrow morning to get some more information?'

'Certainly, Mr Jenkins,' I replied. 'The more publicity we get for the event, the better. We must fill the hall for it.'

'You must be joking, Vicar,' he went on. 'Your trouble is going to be telling people that the tickets are all gone. I bet you any money that you will be sold out as soon as the tickets are ready. Anyway, what time shall I come?'

'Make it eleven o'clock,' I said. 'I have a wedding at twelve.'

When I told Eleanor who had phoned, she said, 'Well, there's something, you won't have any trouble with the headlines this time.'

Prompt at eleven o'clock the next morning, Ed Jenkins arrived with his notepad at the ready. 'I won't keep you long, Vicar. Just a kick-off, as it were. I'll be coming to see you later on to get the family background. We'll need a photograph of you and your brother for that. All I want now are details of the supporting bill, shall we say, and some indication as to when the tickets will be on sale.'

I gave him the details he needed. 'As for the photograph, Mr Jenkins, I shall want an assurance that I will have it back once you have finished with it. I have lost two at least over the past years.'

'Don't worry,' he replied, 'it will be as safe as houses with me. By the way, I've just heard that there has been a nasty accident on the Pontypool road, so if you will excuse me, I must be off to cover it.'

No sooner had he left the Vicarage than the phone rang. It was Eleanor. She was helping out in the emergency ward at the hospital. 'Fred, I think you had better come up here as soon as you can. The Rural Dean has been brought in. He has been badly injured in a road accident. I don't think he has long to live.'

'Right,' I said, 'I'll be up there straight away.' Then I paused. 'Hold on, I've got this wedding at twelve o'clock and it's a quarter past eleven now.'

'Blow the wedding,' she exploded. 'You don't have to stay up here long. If you are a few minutes late, they will understand when you tell them what has happened.'

As I put the phone down, I suddenly thought of Hugh Thomas. If he was still in at his digs in Raglan House, I could get him to take the wedding. I raced down the drive in my Ford 8 and was impeded by the Saturday traffic once I was out on the road. By the time I reached Raglan House, it was twenty-five past eleven. I ran up the steps and rang the bell.

To my great relief Hugh opened the door. 'What's the matter, Vicar?' he exclaimed.

'Can you take the twelve o'clock wedding?' I breathed. 'The Rural Dean has had a terrible accident and I have to be at his bedside as soon as possible.'

'By all means,' he replied. 'I have just been preparing

my sermon for tomorrow. Janet and I are not going out till this afternoon.'

'Good lad,' I said. 'You'll find all the details on the desk in the vestry.'

I fought my way through the traffic, overtaking on the inside when necessary and incurring the wrath of tooting drivers. It was five to twelve when I drove into the hospital car park. I ran into the entrance. The receptionist said, 'There's no need to rush, Vicar. The Reverend Evans is still in the operating theatre. I will let Dr Secombe know you are here.'

A few minutes later Eleanor appeared. 'You had better get back to your wedding, love,' she told me. 'I don't think he will be out of the operating theatre for a while.'

'Hugh Thomas is officiating,' I replied, 'otherwise there would have been a loud chorus of "Why are we waiting?" by the time I would have arrived. More importantly, what is the latest on the Rural Dean's condition?'

'I examined him when he was brought in. The X-rays show that he has a fractured pelvis, some broken ribs, one broken leg and a hairline fracture of the skull. In other words, he is in a mess. The surgeon is doing his best at the moment, but his heart is in a bad condition and I doubt if it will survive the trauma.'

'Poor old man,' I said. 'How about his wife? Was she with him in the car?'

'No, thank God,' replied my wife. 'She would have been killed outright. The passenger side of the car was a tangled mess apparently. The police are contacting her. I expect she will be here very soon. You can be of great assistance then, my love. Take a seat while I get back to my duties.'

As I was musing on the Rural Dean's glossary of invented words, a police car pulled up outside the entrance. A white-faced Mrs Evans was escorted by a police officer. I rose from my seat and went to meet her. I was unable to speak but just held her hand.

'Terrible, isn't it, Mr Secombe?' she said quietly.

'Your husband is still in the operating theatre,' I replied. 'I expect my wife will be with you in a minute and she can tell you what the situation is.'

'If you don't mind,' said the police officer, 'I'll leave you now with the Reverend, Mrs Evans. I'll be back later on.' Meanwhile the receptionist had phoned Eleanor, who took the Rural Dean's wife into a side room as he left. I went back to my seat and prepared myself to comfort the lady. Bronwen Evans was a farmer's daughter, strong as an ox and gentle as a lamb. I admired her greatly as the ideal Vicar's wife. Anyone who coped with the Rural Dean and his idiosyncrasies as well as she did had to be admired.

About a quarter of an hour later, Eleanor came out of the side room. 'She needs your help now, love. I am afraid that her husband has just died.'

I spent an hour with her, listening to her talking of their life together from the time of his curacy to his exaltation as Rural Dean. She was talking her grief away as I listened. No tears were shed. She was a brave woman.

Later that afternoon Eleanor told me how the accident had occurred. The Reverend Llewellyn Evans was a menace on the roads, driving slowly and occasionally on the wrong side. He must have been doing that on a sharp bend in the road and came into collision with a speeding coal lorry. There was no way the lorry driver could have avoided him apparently. 'She is going to be very lonely,' said Eleanor, 'with no children to give her support.'

'I expect she will go back to rural life in Carmarthenshire,' I replied. 'She told me that she has a sister who is a farmer's wife. There's one thing, if she goes to live with her she will find life much more congenial than being closeted in the Vicarage in Llandufrig with no phone to answer and no parishioners to cope with. I don't think she and her husband were very close.'

'You can't say that,' said my wife. 'You weren't a fly on the Vicarage wall. They have meant much more to each other than you think. People may make the same assumption about us.' I was about to remonstrate, then I noticed the twinkle in her eye.

1 2

'Let me repeat, this is a secret ballot, a secret ballot. So don't divulge the name you have written on your piece of paper to your neighbour. Then hand it to the Chapter Clerk when he comes round with the – er – collection box which we are using for the occasion. A secret ballot.'

It was the first Chapter meeting after the death of the Reverend Llewellyn Evans, BA, RD, and the brethren were assembled under the chairmanship of the Archdeacon to cast their votes for the election of a new Rural Dean. The venue was the church hall at Cwmarfon, the only edifice erected in the deanery since the end of the war. It was a cheerless concrete building more suitable as a garage than a meeting place. Already there were leaks in the roof and the low ceiling produced such discomfort in midsummer that it rivalled the Black Hole of Calcutta.

The Vicar was the Reverend Horace Philpott, an ambitious clergyman in his late forties. He sported a goatee beard and his braying voice had been heard flattering every member of the Chapter as they came into the hall. As he shook hands with each newcomer, his eyes were trained on the doorway since the Archdeacon had not yet arrived. Once the dignitary loomed into the entrance, he left his greeting to the Vicar of Penybont in mid-air and made a beeline for him, scattering two groups of gossiping clergy in the process.

When he began to fawn over the Venerable Titus Phillips, Will Evans, Vicar of Llanybedw, known as 'Uncle Will' to Eleanor, indicated to me that he was about to vomit. 'If ever there was a blatant attempt to get promotion, that is it,' he said. 'Already he can see himself as Rural Dean, then Archdeacon and ultimately Archbishop of Wales. I think he is in for a big surprise over his very first step, don't you, Ken?' Ken Williams, Vicar of Aberwain, was standing alongside him. These two men had been my friends ever since I met them in the very hall where this particular Chapter assembly was taking place. 'We've been doing a lot of canvassing over the phone, haven't we?'

The Vicar of Aberwain indulged in a conspiratorial grin. 'You could say that, Will, or, to quote the Archdeacon, you could say that, you certainly could say that.'

'Well,' I said, 'here we are again in the same three seats at the back of the hall as we were in my first Chapter meeting in the deanery.'

'Not to be too unkind to the faithful departed,' commented Will Evans, 'and with the same kind of drip in the chair.'

The meeting had begun with prayers intoned by the Archdeacon, including two for the soul of the departed Rural Dean. Then there followed a fulsome tribute to Llewellyn Evans for 'his firm guidance and his pastoral care of the clergy in the deanery'.

'Who is he talking about?' whispered Uncle Will.

'Now,' said the Archdeacon, 'let us have the minutes of the last meeting.'

The Reverend Tobias Thomas, Vicar of Arfon and Chapter clerk, a dapper portly man, read out what had transpired at the late Rural Dean's swan-song appearance. Tobias would have made an excellent secretary at a board meeting, but his clipped businesslike tones delivering a précis of an inspiring address by a visiting speaker, a hospital chaplain in London, made a sow's ear out of a silk purse.

'Now then,' said the Chairman, 'we come to the purpose of this meeting and that is to elect a new Rural Dean. This is an important post, as you know. Important because the one elected will have to – er, how shall I put it? – take the pulse of the clergy!'

Will Evans suggested, *sotto voce*, that Eleanor should be elected.

'Important too,' droned on the Archdeacon, 'because he will have to – er – galvanize his brothers into action on occasions.'

Ken Williams began to giggle as Will stated that the only galvanizing done in the deanery had been at the works in Llanderi.

'Finally, important too ...' said the Chairman. There was a pause while he thought of his third 'important'.

'Thank God it's "finally",' whispered Will.

'Important,' repeated the Archdeacon, waiting for inspiration, 'because – er –' he paused again, 'he will have to lead by example.'

'That,' said Will, 'is a summary of everything that poor old Llew was not.'

There was an outbreak of conversation as 'Tubby' Tobias took around his collection box. This was then emptied on the table and the counting began. A frown settled on the Archdeacon's forehead when the Chapter clerk reported the result to him. 'I wonder why his venerableness looks so upset,' said Will. 'Perhaps it is because he fears that someone will be appointed who upset him physically recently.'

'We now have two names to present to the Bishop,' announced the Archdeacon. 'Will you all stand for the blessing?'

As the meeting broke up, I said to Uncle Will, 'What did you mean by that remark?'

'My dear Fred,' he replied, 'you are an innocent abroad. Ken and I have been canvassing hard on your behalf. The only person in the deanery who likes Horace Philpott is Horace Philpott. He has convinced himself that he is very popular and the obvious choice as Rural Dean. It seems to us, and to most of the clergy we have phoned, that it is time for someone young and energetic to be the successor to an old and ineffective head man of the deanery. When the Bishop is presented with the two names, I'll bet my bottom dollar that he will ask you to take on the job.'

'That is if my name is one of the two,' I said. 'In any case, I have enough to do in Abergelly without taking on further responsibility.'

'Nonsense!' exploded Will. 'Apart from chairing a few meetings and arranging for services to be taken when there is a vacancy, what is there to do? Believe me, very soon you will have a phone call from his lordship offering you the post.'

He was right. Two days later the Bishop phoned me. 'I am pleased to say that the clergy in your deanery have voted overwhelmingly in your favour as the next Rural Dean. I know you have much to do in Abergelly, but I am sure that with your abundant energy you will be able to cope with this extra responsibility. If you want to think it over before giving me your answer, do so by all means. I hope, for the deanery's sake and indeed your own sake, that you will acknowledge the trust that your fellow clergy have in you.'

When I told Eleanor about the phone call, she was delighted. 'You have told him that you will accept, of course,' she said.

'I did not,' I replied. 'First of all I felt that I should consult you because of the inroads it will make on my time, and second I am not sure that I am experienced enough to be in charge of clergy, all of whom are older than I.'

'What do you mean, "to be in charge of"?' she demanded. 'They are not your curates. You will be just a chairman, that's all. It is more of an honorary appointment than anything. As far as I am concerned, I am sure that I have sufficient to do with my own job without worrying about the "inroads on your time", as you put it. I should love to be the wife of a Rural Dean. So ring him up now and say yes.'

I went into my study and rang the Bishop. 'That was a quick decision, Fred,' he said, 'but a very wise one. There is a meeting of the Rural Deans at my place in a fortnight's time. You will be notified in due course. I shall look forward to seeing you there.'

My wife came in as I put the phone down. 'I have told him that I accept the offer,' I announced.

'Congratulations, Mr Rural Dean,' she said and kissed me.

When I told Tom Beynon and Ivor Hodges at church on Sunday morning of my appointment, they were most effusive. 'Do you know,' said Tom, 'this is the first time ever that the parish has had a Rural Dean as its Vicar. I'll tell you what, you must be the youngest Rural Dean ever in this part of the world.'

Ivor was more pragmatic. 'The first thing we must do now,' he suggested, 'is to add the letters RD to the BA after your name on the church notice board.'

'Does that entitle me to join the Bardic Circle?' I replied.

'The last thing that could be said about Llewellyn Evans was that he was a Bard,' said Ivor. 'I don't think he had an ounce of poetry in his soul. As for you, with your very limited knowledge of the Welsh language, I am afraid you will never enter that band of the Celtic elite. At least you are now part of the clerical elite, if not of the Celtic elite. So that's something.'

'Something indeed!' added Tom. 'Not only that, Vicar, but you are now somebody. We've looked up to you as our Vicar but now you are something more than that.'

I told Eleanor about the conversation at Sunday dinner. 'For heaven's sake, Frederick,' she said, 'don't get big-headed about this. I know I shall like being the Rural Dean's wife, but there is a limit to its importance. As I told you when the Bishop offered you the post, it means you are going to be a chairman and nothing more. It's just that I like the fact that your title has two words to it. Canon, Archdeacon, Dean, Chancellor, are one word only, but

Rural Dean has a musical sound about it, especially when you add the word "Mister" to it. After all, you don't say "Mister Canon".'

'I can assure you,' I replied, 'I have no illusions about my position as Rural Dean, only misgivings. Not only that, but I do not intend to wear a rosette in my hat.'

That afternoon was the first Sunday in the month, when baptisms were held in the afternoon. It was the day when Mr and Mrs Harry Evans informed me that there would be one hundred and twenty in the congregation to witness the christening of Diana Dorothy. There were two other baptisms due to take place. We were finishing our Sunday dinner when there was a ring on the door bell. Mrs Cooper volunteered to answer it to let us have 'a bit of peace', as she put it. 'Shall I send them away?' she asked.

'If it is a tramp, do so by all means,' I said, 'but if it is not come and let me know if it is something urgent.' Back she came with the information that it was Mr Elbow and that he wanted to have the keys to open up the church. I looked at my watch. It was two o'clock and the service was not until three. I arose in high dudgeon and strode down the hall to confront the churchwarden of St David's.

By the time I reached the doorstep my indignation had begun to subside. When I saw Dai's smiling countenance it was near the zero point. 'Good afternoon, Dean,' he said. 'Congratulations on being given such an Honour,' using the aspirate vigorously. 'The Curate told me this morning that you 'ad been promoted, if you know what I mean. I 'ope I'm not too early, like, but I thought I could 'elp with the christenings by giving out those cards, especially since

'Arry Evans said there was over a 'undred coming for 'is do alone.'

'Well, Dai,' I replied, 'on the principle that it is better to be too early rather than too late, that's fine, but I have a feeling that you will be marooned in an empty church for quite a long time.'

'Oh, that's all right, Vicar – I mean Dean,' he said. 'I tell you what, I'll put out the cards in the pews so that they'll 'ave everything in front of them when they get there, otherwise there would be a big rush when they all come in together and I wouldn't know where I was. 'Arry Evans 'as been a good friend of mine for many years. We used to be in school together and 'e lived in our road. In the summer when our gang played cricket on what we called "the patch", a bit of waste ground behind the 'ouses, 'e was the only one who 'ad a real cricket bat. Mind, it 'ad a long 'andle but only 'alf. What was left of the rest of it was covered in black tape. All we 'ad was the bats you could buy in Woolworths, no three splice, just a piece of wood, so we used to bribe 'im for the use of 'is bat. I think that's 'ow he grew up to be a bookie. Sorry to keep you, Vicar, but if you give me the keys I'll go and open the church.'

When I went back into the dining room Eleanor said, 'That's a different face from the one that stormed from the table! How come?'

'Harry Evans' cricket bat,' I replied.

When I went across to the church at a quarter to three I expected to see a crowd queuing up to get into the church. Instead there was a mere handful of people outside. When I went into the nave I found Dai in earnest conversation with a couple and no more than about forty people in the pews. I went into the vestry and filled the gleaming brass ewer with water. As I stood pouring the water into the imposing stone font at the front of the church, suddenly there was an influx of a loud-mouthed crowd of spectators breathing alcoholic fumes and destroying the serenity of the house of God. I made my escape and retreated into the vestry where I remained until three o'clock.

From the noise which greeted me when I emerged, it could have been Saturday at Chepstow Racecourse. I went up into the pulpit and surveyed the scene. The total congregation could not have been more than seventy. In the front pew were Mr and Mrs Harry Evans plus Diana Dorothy, cradled in her mother's arms and pacified with a large dummy. The young Mrs Evans was sporting the fur coat she wore when she came to make the arrangements for the christening. However, the polka dot dress was replaced by a white flimsy creation, low cut and revealing a considerable amount of her ample bosom, since once again the fur coat adorned only her shoulders.

Occupying the rest of the pew were the two godparents, an elderly gentleman who looked as if he would depart this life long before the baby would be old enough to be confirmed and the godmothers, apparently in their teens, wearing the mini skirts which had just come into fashion. Right behind them were three pews of race-goers, by their appearance and demeanour. At the back of the church were the other two candidates for baptism, sheltered in the arms of their mothers, who were soberly dressed and evidently disconcerted by the presence of the rowdy element at the forefront of the congregation. I waited for the hubbub to die down.

'May I welcome you all into St Peter's Church,' I began. 'You have come here this afternoon to witness one of the most important occasions in the lives of these three babies. They are about to become members of Christ, children of God and inheritors of the Kingdom of Heaven.' These sentiments were ignored by the Harry Evans contingent who were passing sweets around and indulging in whispered conversations.

Confronted by this spectacle of complete indifference, my hackles rose, as did my voice. 'Why, in God's name,' I exclaimed, 'are some of you sitting here as if nothing is happening, as if it is Saturday in the cinema or a serial on television? What is happening here later on is God bursting into this world and entering the lives of the three children who will be brought to the font. I want you and especially the godparents and even more especially the parents, to realize that this is not just something to be read from a card, that solemn promises will be made which will affect these young lives until the time comes when they will return to God who created them.'

By now there was complete silence. The sweets stayed in pockets and all heads were turned towards the pulpit. For the next five minutes, in simple English, I explained the significance of Holy Baptism. Then I said, 'Will the godparents and parents please come to the front of the church and stand by the font. You will find the service beginning at the top of the baptismal card.'

There was another outbreak of conversation as the godparents and parents made their way to the side of the font. In the forefront were Harry Evans and company. Shirley Evans delivered the sleeping child into the arms of the elder teenager, after a number of complicated manoeuvres. 'See you keep 'er 'ead up.' Miraculously the baby remained asleep throughout the handover. In the meanwhile, the other two baptismal parties arranged themselves behind the Harry Evans front line.

'Will the congregation remain seated, please,' I shouted, 'and follow the service on the card, joining in the prayer halfway down the second column.' The muted responses of the godparents were almost inaudible. When it came to the baptism, some of the bookmaker's supporters began to stand on the seats.

'Before I begin to christen these children, will you all *please* stay in the pews and not stand on them!' I shouted yet again. Once again there was a silence.

'Give the baby to the Vicar,' instructed Shirley Evans.

The young girl wrapped up the infant in the shawl. I was presented with a bundle of clothing with no human form visible. As I attempted to find the baby, I said, 'Name this child.' By now I had uncovered the face of the child. In the meanwhile there was a silence from the godmother.

'Come on, our Marlene,' rendered the bookie's wife. 'Tell the Vicar.'

'Diana Dorothy,' whispered Marlene. As the cold water from the font besprinkled the brow of the candidate for baptism, Diana Dorothy awakened from her slumber and announced to the world that she was now a new creature with a loud triumphant cry, which dislodged her dummy and echoed around St Peter's. By the time I had made the sign of the cross on her forehead, she had made it fully apparent that she was a force to be reckoned with in the world, with a presence that could never be ignored. The other two baptisms were conducted with the minimum of noise and the ultimate in decorum.

Once inside the vestry, I was confronted with the last two baptisms who were allowed to give their details by Harry Evans, who stood aside as they came forward to register their children's godparents and to receive their baptismal certificates. I wondered why this deference was shown by someone who was not accustomed to be among the also rans. It was soon apparent.

'Thank you, Vicar,' he said. 'That was most enjoyable. Would you please accept this donation to your funds? We would like you to come to the – er – festivities in the British Legion Club, even if it is only for a quick drink, wouldn't we Shirley?'

Shirley was still engaged in pacifying her vociferous child, who was still annoyed that her sleep had been interrupted. 'Oh yes, Vicar. You must come and see this wonderful cake we've 'ad made. It's cost nearly fifty pounds and it's a picture of a baby, all done in icing over the cake. You can have a lift with us down to the Legion, can't 'e, 'Arry?'

'Of course, Vicar,' said her husband.

There was no escape. I sat in the front seat of Harry's Jaguar while he apologized for the fact that they had not been to church since they came to see me about the christening. 'We were coming last Sunday, weren't we, Shirl? We were all ready to come when the baby had a bout of wind, didn't she, Shirl?'

Shirley attested to the fact that Diana Dorothy had been laid low with a stomach complaint which had culminated in a bout of vomiting. 'All over my polka dot frock, wasn't it, 'Arry?'

'Well, here we are, Vicar,' announced the bookmaker as we drove into the car park adjoining the British Legion hut. As we entered the 'club' the noise was deafening. Evidently the eighty absentees had been enjoying themselves while we were in church.

'Come and 'ave a look at this, Vicar,' said the proud mother. The next minute she screeched, 'Oh my God! Someone's eaten 'er 'ead off!!' In front of us was the headless corpse of the fifty-pound masterpiece. Shirley began to wail while her husband sought to comfort her.

A shamefaced man came up to the couple. 'Sorry about this,' he mumbled. 'While we was all up at the bar enjoying a drink, like, some of the kids got to work on the cake. It wasn't until some of them started playing around with lumps of cake in their 'ands that we realized what had happened.'

At this stage, Dai Elbow intervened in a show of righteous indignation. 'If you lot 'ad been in church instead of boozing 'ere on the cheap, it wouldn't 'ave 'appened.'

'I tell you what,' said Harry Evans to his wailing wife, 'I'll get that shop in Cardiff to repair it and we'll just have the family and a few friends around so that you can cut the cake.' This suggestion had an immediate effect on the distraught Shirley. Her loud grief subsided and diminished into a few isolated quiet sobs. It was the signal for a renewal of noisy conversation and a frantic running around by the culprits of the beheading.

After a quarter of an hour, drinking a large whisky, I decided to escape from the crescendo of volume filling the building, which was known locally as 'Noah's Ark'.

'Aren't you going to have some food first, Vicar?' enquired the bookmaker. He pointed to the array of sandwiches, cakes and sausage rolls on the table beside the headless baby.

'Thank you very much, Mr Evans,' I replied, 'but I have to get back ready for Evensong. I am most grateful for your donation to the church funds and for your hospitality.'

'If you will wait a moment I'll drive you back to the Vicarage.'

'There's no need for that,' I said. 'It's not far to walk.'

Once again Dai Elbow made his presence felt. 'It's all right 'Arry, I'll take the Vicar back. After all, 'e is my responsibility as churchwarden.'

As we drove back to the Vicarage in his dilapidated Ford, I said to him, 'Tell me, Dai, who were the godparents? It seems to me that the two godmothers were Shirley's sisters, but who on earth was that elderly gentleman who was the godfather?'

'Oh!' replied Dai. 'That's Levi Goldstein, the big bookie in Cardiff. 'Arry used to work for 'im before 'e branched out on 'is own. Always been a great friend of 'Arry's.'

'How on earth can he be a godfather in a Christian ceremony?' I asked.

'Don't worry, Vicar,' he assured me, ''e is a very religious man for a bookie, a big man in 'is synagogue in Cardiff. 'E'll look after Diana Dorothy, believe me. Mind, I think 'e'll be dead by the time she is confirmed.' He paused in his information. 'That's if she ever gets confirmed!'

When I arrived at the Vicarage, Eleanor met me before I could open the front door. 'Well,' she demanded, 'how did it go?'

'I think the best answer to your question,' I said, 'is that it was a most bewildering afternoon. It began with a greatly reduced congregation from the numbers predicted by Harry and Shirley and ended with a tragedy, involving a decapitated sculpture in the British Legion!'

'Please explain yourself, dear Frederick,' she replied. 'You speak in riddles. It sounds intriguing.'

'Before I do that, my dear,' I said, 'allow me to open this envelope containing the donation to the church funds which Harry Evans presented to me in the vestry.'

I whistled as I looked at the amount on the cheque. One hundred pounds stared me in the face. Eleanor took it from my hand. 'No wonder you whistled,' she commented. 'I would have sung the "Hallelujah Chorus" if I were you. You must keep in close touch with Mr Harry Evans. He is a force to be reckoned with. Let's hope that Shirley will bring forth more progeny.'

'I don't think that will happen, my dear,' I replied. 'I am pretty sure that Diana Dorothy will grow up to be the most spoilt only child in Abergelly. However, as you say, the church has found another potential source of income, thanks to the dynamic churchwarden of St David's Church.'

The next source of income, the Midnight Matinée, was responsible for a plethora of phone calls from aspiring stars in show business. From the moment that news of my brother's appearance at the Miners' Welfare Hall had become known, it seemed that the valleys were bursting with latent talent anxious to be given a showcase for its manifestation. Inevitably, in Abergelly it was Willie James who was offering the services of his scout troop. According to him he had been training them to sing.

'Vicar, they are tremendous, as good as the Luton Girls Choir, or that famous boys' choir in Austria. They've only got five pieces in their repertoire at the moment, but you would only need them to sing a couple in the Harry Secombe show, wouldn't you? Their two best are "Nymphs and Shepherds Come Away" and "Abide with Me".'

'Who is playing the piano for you, Willie?' I asked.

'I am,' he replied.

'Then who is conducting them?'

'I am,' he said proudly. 'I am conducting them from the piano. You just come and hear them.'

'Sorry, Willie,' I told him, 'but the programme has already been arranged. As a matter of fact, the details are with the printers.'

When I told Eleanor of the conversation she was highly amused. 'It's a wonder that he did not offer his services as a soloist with a performance of "On the Road to Mandelay",' she said. 'In any case, I had no idea that he could play the piano.'

'I would think it would be a one-finger exercise,' I replied, 'and even that would be uncertain.'

The Willie James episode had occurred after Evensong on the day of the Diana Dorothy baptism. Two days later I had a phone call from the Archdeacon. 'I am sorry to trouble you, Vicar,' he said with relish, 'but I am afraid I have to – er – impinge on your busy life so soon after your appointment as Rural Dean. The Rector of Cwmsadarn has been taken to hospital with bladder bother of some kind and will be out of commission, shall we say, for some time. This means that you will have to arrange for the services to be taken in the parish until he returns. They are Holy Communion at eight o'clock, eight o'clock, Matins at eleven o'clock, eleven o'clock and Evensong at six thirty, six thirty. Have you got that? I shall repeat it just once more. Holy Communion at eight o'clock, Matins at eleven o'clock and Evensong at six thirty.' Having indulged in his Trinitarian formula, he put the phone down without a word of congratulation on my appointment and, more importantly, without any indication of where I could recruit the necessary assistance to fill the gap in the parish's Sunday timetable.

I took the Diocesan handbook from its place by the telephone. One of the first actions on my appointment as Rural Dean was to have all available information ready to consult. I turned to the list of retired clergy and immediately noted the telephone number of Joseph Morris, who had been my predecessor in Abergelly. Joseph Morris was a kind but ineffective soul, who had vegetated in his parish for more than thirty years. I dialled the number. 'Canon Morris here,' came the basso profondo tones at the other end.

'This is Fred Secombe speaking,' I said.

'Hello, dear boy. How nice to hear you. I hear great things about your work in Abergelly,' came the reply, 'and by the way, congratulations on your appointment as Rural Dean. That is something I never achieved in all the time I was there. Now then, what can I do for you?'

'Well, it is something to do with my elevation,' I said. 'Apparently Evan Bevan at Cwmsadarn has been rushed into hospital with prostate trouble and I have to be responsible for the conduct of the services in the parish.'

'That's one of the millstones around the Rural Dean's neck,' he replied. 'If you are asking me whether I can take the services, I am looking after the parish of Llantilir and have been for the last twelve months, believe it or not, while the Diocesan Board is making its mind up whether it should be incorporated in the parish of Abergwili next door. Why don't you try Canon Edwin Morgan? As far as I know, he is not engaged in any duty at the moment.'

'Thank you, Canon,' I said, 'but I am afraid that if I ask him, I shall get a very dusty answer. As you know, he resides in Abergelly. When he came here, he showed every sign of wanting to take over the parish. On finding that I was fully capable of being in charge without his assistance, he informed me that his ministrations would be directed elsewhere.'

'That's typical of Edwin,' commented my predecessor. 'However, if he thinks that there is a steady income from doing duty in a parish which will be without its incumbent for a considerable length of time, he may swallow his pride. He has always been prepared to compromise with Mammon if it is to his advantage.'

I took a deep breath and dialled Canon Edwin Morgan. After what seemed to be an eternity, I had a reply. 'Canon Morgan shpeaking.'

'Good morning, Canon,' I said. 'This is the Rural Dean. I wonder if you are available to take services at

Cwmsadarn for the next few months or so. The Rector has been taken to hospital with prostate trouble.'

I waited for the dusty answer I had prophesied. There was a long pause. 'Congratsh on your promotion, young man,' said the Canon. 'Yesh indeed, I can oblige. Ash I told you shome time ago, I am only too ready to help where I can. I take it that I shtart next Shunday.'

Suddenly I realized what it meant to have a rise in my station. Even Canon Edwin Morgan was ready to bow the knee.

13

'Dad! Please can I go to Uncle Harry's concert?' pleaded David.

'And me?' shouted Elspeth.

'You can't come,' said my son scornfully, 'you're too young.'

'Now listen, both of you,' I warned them, 'this is the umpteenth time that you have asked me this question and I don't want to hear it again. I have told you that it is far too late for you to be out. So let there be an end to it. You can talk to your uncle when he comes here before the concert. I am sure he will tell you the same as I have told you. You are both much too young to be up at that time.'

David pouted his longest pout. 'What does umpteenth time mean, Daddy?' enquired Elspeth.

It was three weeks before the Midnight Matinée and all the tickets had been sold out on the first day that they were available. Since I had been plagued by requests from everywhere between Newport and Cardiff, I was in no mood to be pestered by my children. As I was explaining to Elspeth what umpteenth meant, the phone rang. My hackles rose when I heard the voice. They had been rising throughout the day, but nothing compared with the height they reached on being approached by the Archdeacon. From his very first words I realized that he was doing a gloat.

'Sorry to trouble you again, Vicar,' he breathed. 'I am afraid that yet another of the clergy in the deanery, the Rector of Cwmdulais, has been laid low with a heart attack. It sounds rather serious. I should imagine he will be out of commission for quite a while, so could you inform the people's warden of the name of the priest who will fill in, shall we say? The warden's name is Mr Arthur Willis, Arthur Willis, 10 Church Avenue, 10 Church Avenue, Cwmdulais, Cwmdulais. Now then, have you got it? Mr Arthur Willis, 10 Church Avenue, Cwmdulais. I am sure that the Rector would appreciate a visit from you at the Royal Gwent Hospital, the Royal Gwent. I can't remember the ward but I am sure they will let you know which one at the information desk. The Royal Gwent.' Then he put the phone down before I could ask any questions.

'Vengeance is mine, I will repay, saith the Archdeacon,' I muttered. Ever since he had made a fool of himself at his visitation by falling over the carpet in my church, he had regarded me as a menace. With years ahead of me as the new Rural Dean, I could foresee trouble any time I had dealings with him. It was not a pleasing prospect.

I went to my desk and thumbed through the diocesan handbook, looking for the list of retired clergy. Most of them I did not know as I read through the roll-call of the faithful servants sent out to graze. The few who were familiar to me were augmenting their pension income with doing what Dai Elbow would describe as 'a hobble' – in other words, gainfully employed in an unofficial role. There were four names left to me. I decided I would approach these gentlemen in alphabetical order.

First on the list was the Reverend Thomas Arthur Davies, 14 Elm Tree Close, Aberglau. I turned to my telephone directory to discover his telephone number. A diligent perusal bore no fruit. Next was the Reverend William Gilbert Grace, evidently the child of a cricket lover. The address was The Cedars, Singleton Drive, Penylan. This time I was successful in unearthing a number. I waited some minutes for a reply to my call, but to no avail. By now I was indulging in one of Hitler's pet phrases, 'My patience is being exhausted.'

The third name was the Reverend Herbert Evan Powell, 23 Twn-y-dail Avenue, Caerddu. This time, to my delight, there was a number. To my even greater delight, my call was answered instantly.

'Herbert Powell speaking,' came the reply.

'The Rural Dean here,' I announced with all the aplomb I could muster.

'Good morning, Mr Rural Dean, and what can I do for you?'

I detected faint signs of mockery in the tones of the Reverend Herbert Powell. I felt that I should have to descend from the exalted pitch of my opening words. It was obvious that my normal manner would be more acceptable to my listener.

'Good morning, Mr Powell,' I said, 'I wonder if you can help me.'

'If I can,' came the unmocking reply.

'The Rector of Cwmdulais has been laid low with a heart attack and will be unavailable for duty for a few months. I am urgently in need of someone who could help out in this situation. I wonder if you would be able to oblige.'

'Well, Mr Rural Dean,' said the Reverend Herbert Powell, 'as it happens, I can oblige, as you put it. My wife and I were about to embark on one of those journeys of a lifetime, as the holiday blurb describes it. However, on further examination of our financial situation, we decided that unless we were stranded on a desert island without any demands on our pockets, we would spend the rest of our lives in abject poverty in a world where mammon was king. So then, how can I help you?'

When I put the phone down, I gave thanks for the Reverend Herbert Evan Powell. An Oxford graduate who had served his apprenticeship in parishes in the Church in Wales and transferred his allegiance to the Church of England, he had ended his ministry as a Vicar of a parish in Bournemouth. He had decided to come back to his ancestral roots in Wales since his wife had strong family connections there and he himself had been brought up in a Vicarage in Pembrokeshire. He promised to take over the duties in Cwmdulais until the Rector came back to the parish.

The one thing which had given me encouragement was his forecast that I would be an effective Rural Dean. 'How good to hear someone who speaks in plain English and not the invented vocabulary of a partly anglicized Welshman.'

Half an hour later Eleanor came in, stressed by a busy morning on the housing estate and looking forward to a relaxed lunch and conversation in the company of her husband. 'I tell you what,' she said as we sat down to a

Mrs Cooper special, baked potatoes and corned beef, 'before long I must have an assistant. Where in God's name he or she will operate I do not know. Either we shall have to get a loan to build a surgery instead of a council house, or erect a tent in the back garden at Brynfelin.'

'I tell you what,' I replied, 'either I shall have to be given a second curate or I shall have to give up any idea of building a new church to replace the prefab. I have only been functioning for a few weeks and already responsibilities begin to appear. Should there be another hospital case or a vacancy in a parish, then it will mean that Hugh Thomas and I will have to fill in.'

'The only thing we can do, Mr Rural Dean,' said my wife, 'is to follow the advice from the Sermon on the Mount, which you give to your congregation frequently. Let us take everything a day at a time. Each day has troubles enough of its own, as the new translation puts it. "Physician, heal thyself."'

'Thank you, Reverend Doctor,' I grunted. 'You can preach the sermon next Sunday.'

That afternoon was my once-a-month sick visiting of the chronically ill who were not confirmed. I spent some time with two old ladies and a very elderly gentleman who was hoping to last out the few remaining months of his century. The matron of the old people's home told me that the only topic of his conversation was his expected telegram from the Queen. 'Once he gets that,' she said, 'that is, if he does get it, I am sure he will be dead the next day. Isn't it strange that a piece of paper can do more to prolong life than several bottles of medicine?'

My last visit was to Joe Davies, a World War II victim of service with the Eighth Army in the deserts of North Africa. Both his legs had fallen prey to the extremes of temperature when he had been wounded. Two of the fingers on his right hand had disappeared, so he taught himself to become left-handed, yet despite all this, whenever I came to see him, trapped in his wheelchair, I was always greeted with a smile. He had a dedicated wife who had nursed him when he was in hospital. Sometimes he was in severe pain but her skilled ministrations were his lifeline. This afternoon he opened the door to me after a while, apologizing for the length of time involved and explaining that Miriam was out shopping. He preceded me into the parlour and motioned me to sit down in the chintz-covered armchair by the window.

'My wife will be back soon,' he informed me. 'Anyway, I'm glad she is not here at the moment. I have something I would like to ask you that she doesn't know anything about. For quite a while I have been thinking that I should be confirmed. She is regular at Holy Communion, as you are aware. I would not be able to come to church, it would be too inconvenient, but I would like to share the sacrament with Miriam. What worries me is how I get confirmed.'

'Before you go any further, Joe,' I said, 'let me say that this is great news. I shall have a word with the Bishop to see if he will come here to the house to confirm you.'

His deep-lined face broke into a radiant smile. 'Do you think he will?' he asked. 'It's a bit much to expect him to do a one-off, as it were.'

'Our Bishop is a very kind man,' I replied, 'and I feel sure that when we have our confirmation at St Peter's

Church next March, he will come here, either before or after, to lay his hands on your head.'

'Thank you, Vicar,' he said. 'You don't know how much that means to me.'

When Miriam came in with her shopping some time later, he announced to her his intention to be confirmed. She went to him and kissed him, running her hands through his shock of silver-white hair. It was a while before she could speak. 'This is wonderful, isn't it, Vicar?' she said.

'Next Easter,' I told her, 'you and Joe will be able to have your Easter Communion together in your own home. When I come on my monthly visit, I will give you some instruction and I shall give Miriam a booklet for you when she comes to church next Sunday.'

'My word!' exclaimed Eleanor when she came in from her surgery. 'You look a lot happier than you did at lunchtime. Who waved the magic wand?'

'Someone called Joe Davies,' I replied. 'He wants to be confirmed.'

'Splendid!' said my wife, 'But how on earth can he get down to church. He never goes out.'

'I have told him that I shall get the Bishop to come to his home to confirm him,' I told her. 'I am sure that he will. As a matter of fact, I shall ring him once we have had our dinner. I tell you one thing, talking with Joe Davies has put my worries into a proper perspective. There is a serenity about the man which makes me feel small in his presence.'

'Thank God for Joe Davies,' proclaimed Eleanor, 'and all those like him.'

Once David and Elspeth had gone to bed, I went into the study to phone his lordship. I told him the circumstances concerning Joe's request for confirmation. 'I wondered whether you would visit his home when you come for the parish confirmation in March,' I said.

'By all means,' said the Bishop. 'Better still, I am holding a confirmation service at Llangwn in mid-December. As it is next door to your parish, why don't we arrange for a service for your Joe Davies that day? In that case, he will be able to have his first Christmas Communion with his wife in their own home.'

'What a wonderful man,' commented Eleanor when I told her the result of my conversation.

'And what a pity that he is near retirement age,' I added. 'I dread to think who might replace him. Just imagine having our trinitarian Archdeacon as our Father in God!'

'Nobody in their right senses would vote for him in the electoral college,' exploded my wife.

'Stranger things have happened,' I said.

'Frederick, you are pulling my leg,' she retorted. 'That would not be strange, that would be catastrophic.'

The next two weeks seemed to fly past. The Sunday before the Friday of the Midnight Matinée had arrived, and excitement in the parish about my brother's appearance on the stage of the Miners' Welfare Hall was reaching fever pitch. Attendance at the Family Communion service was exceptionally high for the Sunday next before Advent.

'It's a pity you couldn't arrange for him to put on a show more frequently,' commented Eleanor. 'Just imagine what that would do for your Communion figures, apart from the parish finances.'

'Excuse me, my dear,' I retorted, 'I don't see why I should exploit Harry to do my work to raise money for the new church when it is my responsibility and not his.'

'Well,' she replied, 'he uses you as his private chaplain to do his children's baptisms, let alone his own wedding service. Not only that, but it must do something for his public image to have a man of the cloth as his brother, even if he does call you the black sheep of the family.'

'All I can say,' I said, 'is that you sound very cynical for a Vicar's wife.'

'That's not cynicism,' she rejoined, 'but a statement of fact. What's more, don't put on that holier-than-thou act. It doesn't become you. You know perfectly well that what I have said is true. He owes you much more than you owe him.'

We were enjoying a postprandial drink in the sitting room after a splendid roast beef Sunday dinner supplied by Mrs Cooper at her culinary best. The children were upstairs in the playroom, where a noisy argument was percolating down from above. 'It seems that they don't agree, either,' I said.

'Look, Frederick,' replied my wife, 'I don't wish to argue, but I was simply pointing out that even though you have chosen a completely different path in life from that pursued by your illustrious brother, you are just as important in your own way as he is and you don't owe him any favours. You are in constant contact with your parishioners. Your are either on their doorstep or they are on yours. They are not the public, but individuals who know you as their Father in God. You are with them in all the great occasions of their lives – birth, marriage and death, not to mention the times of sickness that intervene. Don't devalue the importance of your ministry, my love. You are doing something which he could never emulate. In my eyes, as another servant of the people, your contribution is worth far more to them than a radio programme or a gramophone record. So lift up your heart.'

I kissed her.

That evening after Evensong, Graham Webb was rehearsing his ad hoc orchestra in the church hall. My brother's band parts had arrived by special delivery the previous Thursday. Elizabeth Williams was there to have a run-through of her solos with Graham at the piano. 'I'm terrified already,' she told me. 'What I shall be like on Friday, I dread to think.'

'Have a glass of whisky before you go on stage,' advised Tom Beynon.

'Since I don't drink, Mr Beynon,' she replied, 'I'm afraid that would make matters worse, not better.'

'Don't worry, Elizabeth,' I said, 'you are supposed to be nervous before you appear before the public. Harry is always nervous, and believe me, he will be even more nervous next Friday because he will be helping his brother. In any case, a certain amount of nervousness always gives an edge to the performance. You know that from our Gilbert and Sullivan epic a few months ago. Everybody was petrified – apart from Willie James, that is, and you know how his smugness almost wrecked the policemen's entrance. He even wanted to conduct his Scouts in an item on the programme for the Midnight Matinée: "Nymphs and

Shepherds, Come Away" and "Abide with Me". As Eleanor said, she didn't know whether it was an offer of accommodation at his council house to the bucolic group or simply a song and a hymn.'

'Talk of the devil,' said Tom, 'here he comes.'

Dressed in his Sunday best, Willie swaggered up to the three of us. 'Good evening, all!' he greeted us, in a pathetic attempt to mimic Jack Warner's policeman by someone who was barely five feet tall. 'Going well, is it?'

'Very well indeed,' I replied. 'What can I do for you?'

'I was wondering whether the Scouts can help on Friday by selling programmes,' he said. 'As you know, we shall be meeting here tomorrow night. I can organize them into sections, Vicar, quite easily. You know the sort of thing. Some outside the doors of the Welfare and some in the hall.'

'My dear Willie,' I replied, 'arrangements for pro- gramme selling and for ushering were made some two months ago.'

'Just wanted them to feel they were part of the church,' he said huffily.

'All I can say to that,' I retorted, 'is that if they want to feel part of the church they should come to it every Sunday, not only on church parades. Even then half of them are missing on those occasions.'

His face dropped. Suddenly I felt sorry for the little man. 'I tell you what, Willie,' I added, 'if they were as reg- ular in church-going as their Scoutmaster, they really would be part of the church.'

'Thank you, Vicar,' he said, 'for that compliment. I do try my best with the boys, but since their parents don't come to worship, they don't see any reason why they should, either. Anyway, I shall keep on plugging away at them. I suppose if only two or three started to come regularly that would be something.'

'I would think that would be quite an achievement, Scoutmaster,' I replied. He went away with a smile on his face.

'He doesn't get much encouragement,' commented Tom Beynon. 'I think he needed that.'

As the orchestra was playing some of my brother's hit numbers, another visitor entered the hall. Ricky Parker, a comedian described in the local press as 'a rising young comic', came up to me as I was talking to Tom and Elizabeth.

'Could I have a few words with you in private, Vicar?' he asked. He was wearing the statutory ankle-length coat and was sporting a blue bow tie on his pink shirt.

'By all means,' I replied, and took him into one of the side rooms.

'I expect Harry will be coming to the Vicarage before he goes to the Welfare Hall,' he began.

'I suppose so,' I said.

'Well,' he went on, 'I hope you don't think I have a great cheek, but I wonder if I could have a few words with him at your place. I know what it will be like once he is down there. I won't stand a cat in hell's chance of speaking to him privately, if you will excuse the language, Vicar. All I want to do is to ask him to advise me on who is the best agent I can get to represent me. The bloke I've got at the moment only covers the valleys, with an occasional concert in Cardiff and that's it. If I want to get on in show business, I'll have to find someone with big names on his books.'

A little bell rang in my head, warning me that I should not be a 'soft touch', to use my wife's description of me. 'I'm afraid it will be a family occasion for an hour or so,' I replied. 'It is very rarely that I see him. Not only that, but he is bringing his pianist with him and he might like to have a run over some of his songs, so I can hardly see how he can fix an interview with you in such a tight schedule.'

I thought that would put him off. I was wrong.

'All I want, Vicar, is a couple of minutes. My whole career could hang on those few minutes. As a man of the cloth, I'm sure you can see what that means to me. All I need is a name and a telephone number.'

I paused before replying. His face changed: he could see a chink in my armour of non-compliance. 'Well,' I said, taking a long time over the word, 'if you come about six o'clock on Friday evening, I'll see what I can do for you. It's not certain that he will want to see you, anyway.' He shook my hand vigorously, told me I was a saint and made a rapid exit.

When I went back into the hall, the orchestra had finished their rehearsal. Graham Webb looked quite pleased. 'I think we can do a reasonable job for your brother,' he said. 'It's a pity we could not get a few more in the brass section, but there you are. What we have are all of them quite competent. Now then, Elizabeth, let's get down to your contribution.'

I sat at the back with Tom Beynon and listened to Handel, Purcell and the Welsh love song 'Myfanwy'. We clapped each rendition fervently. As Tom said, 'That should give her heart for next Friday.'

Eleanor was watching television when I came into the sitting room. She switched it off and asked for an appraisal of the rehearsal. 'Splendid!' I enthused. 'I'm sure Harry will be well pleased with the orchestra, and Elizabeth's solos were excellent. It should be a great show.'

'By the way,' she said, 'he rang while you were out. He said he would be arriving at the Vicarage some time after seven o'clock. He doesn't want a meal before the concert, but he would be grateful for something after the "do".'

I frowned. 'What's the matter?' she asked.

I took a deep breath. 'While I was at the hall,' I said, 'Ricky Parker, that young comedian we saw at the Rotary Club concert the other day, came in to – er – find out if he could have a brief word with Harry about – er – suggesting a good agent for him.'

She gave me one of her hard looks. 'Yes,' she murmured. 'Go on.'

'He was so persistent,' I went on. 'I tried to put him off but he made it appear that his whole future depended on whether I would let him have a brief word with my brother.' I sighed. 'So I told him he could come here at six o'clock.'

'Secombe!' she said, in a tone of voice which would have frozen the boldest of adversaries. 'You must be the most gullible of all gulls, if there is such a name for humans. Your poor brother will arrive here after several hours' journey. He has an audience who bought tickets to hear him two months ago and hundreds of others who would give their right arm to be there, and you are quite prepared to let a tuppenny-ha'penny comic pester him in what little time he has to rest. I don't believe it.

It's a jolly good thing you told him to come at six o'clock. So you will be able to tell him that Harry is not here and that what little time he has left will be spent with his family.'

An uneasy peace settled upon the Vicarage, that is if a peace can ever be uneasy. For two days meals were eaten in comparative silence. Then on Wednesday, to my great surprise and even greater embarrassment, a soberly dressed Ricky Palmer presented himself at the altar rails to receive the sacrament at mid-week Holy Communion. I stayed in the vestry for some time after the service, forgoing my normal practice of shaking hands at the church door with the communicants. After ten minutes or so I came out into the sanctuary to remove the vessels from the credence table. To my dismay, I could see Ricky at the back of the church, loitering with grim intent, as far as I was concerned. There was no escape. I waved feebly with one hand as I carried the tray into the vestry. I put away the chalice and paten in the safe and I walked down to meet him with a sickly smile upon my countenance.

'Hello, Ricky,' I said. 'What a pleasant surprise and what a welcome addition to our communicant numbers. Do you live in the parish?'

'I'm afraid not,' he replied. 'I live in Newport now but I used to be a server at Cwmgwili when I was a lad. I don't go to church much these days, so it was a joy to take part in the service today. Not only that, but it gave me an opportunity to dedicate what talent I have to our Lord and Saviour. I wanted to see you to check on the time I am supposed to come to the Vicarage, to see if your brother had changed the arrangements, perhaps.'

I swallowed hard. 'As a matter of fact, Ricky,' I said, 'he has. It seems now that he will not be arriving until seven o'clock at the earliest. That doesn't give him much time with us. I would suggest that you speak with him at the Welfare Hall after the show. I shall see that you will be given the five minutes you want with him, I promise you.'

His face fell. 'Thank you, Vicar,' he replied. 'Beggars can't be choosers. I know what it is like in dressing rooms after a show. That's why I thought a quiet word with him in the Vicarage would be more fruitful. There you are, c'est la vie, as the actress said to the Bishop. See you on Friday evening, Vicar.'

His was a different exit from the church compared to the excited dash from the church hall.

I decided I would not mention my second meeting with the comedian to Eleanor. 'A still tongue keeps a wise head,' I said to myself. It was an adage which did not come naturally to me. At Matins on Friday morning, I prayed for God's blessing on the evening's big event, which was due to begin at eleven o'clock that night. As we unrobed in the vestry, Hugh Thomas reported to me that Brynfelin's main topic of conversation was Harry's appearance at the Miners' Welfare Hall.

'For weeks I have been plugging the message that he was coming to help build the church on the estate,' he said. 'He is coming to help Brynfelin, not Abergelly, I have told them. Dai Elbow has been telling everybody that your brother is looking forward to the day when the church will be consecrated and that most likely he will be there to sing in the service. I wish all this excitement would lead to a big increase in church attendance, but I'm afraid that our congregations have shown only a marginal rise in numbers.'

'My dear Hugh,' I replied, 'All we can do is to give of our best and then leave the rest to the Almighty. To quote an outworn cliché, "Rome wasn't built in a day." '

When I went down to the Miners' Welfare Hall in the afternoon, I found an army of ladies decorating the window-sills with an array of flowers. On the stage was a frontage worthy of a Covent Garden presentation, and directing all the proceedings was Mrs Lily Whitehouse of 'Floral Perfection', Abergelly's High Street premier flower shop. Lily was a regular at the parish church early Communion. A widow in her early sixties, she was a dynamo dedicated to her trade, finding satisfaction in what had been a childless marriage by selling and arranging flowers.

'Now then, Vicar,' she demanded as she stood in the central aisle, 'how about that for a setting worthy of a star of your brother's reputation?'

'Mrs Whitehouse,' I said, 'you take my breath away. It's fabulous. That's the only word to describe it.'

'Flattery will get you nowhere, Vicar,' she replied, 'but you are quite right. I was down at the station at six o'clock this morning with our old crock of a van and I must have unloaded half a trainful of flowers. Anyway, it's worth all that trouble to see the result this afternoon. What's more, I am not charging you anything. It is my donation to the Brynfelin Church Building Fund.'

I gave her a hug. 'You are a lovely woman,' I declared.

'Now then, Vicar,' she said, 'stop that! What will your wife say when she hears what all these gossips will tell her? You've made them stop their decorating for a bit of scandal.'

'I'm sure she will say, in the words of the gossip columnist, "It is purely platonic",' I replied.

'Knowing Dr Secombe, I am positive that is what she would say. She knows she's got a good 'un in you,' she said.

Eleanor's car was in the Vicarage drive when I returned. The children had come home from school and were in a ferment of excitement, which had affected Lulu. The dog was prancing around the house like a demented creature. As I came in through the front door, she jumped at me in an attempt to kiss me. 'Down, dog!' I exclaimed.

'She is only loving you, Daddy,' explained Elspeth.

My wife came out of the kitchen. 'Frederick,' she said, in her ominously quiet voice, 'this house is in urgent need of some kind of control. So far I have not been able to do anything about it. So over to you. I am going back to help Mrs Cooper prepare a meal for tonight.'

David came rushing through the passage to join Elspeth and Lulu in a rugby scrum, more appropriate to Cardiff Arms Park than a Vicarage. 'Calm down!' I screamed in my loudest tones. 'What will your Uncle Harry think of you? He'll pack his bags and go back home, and then we shan't have our concert tonight.' This brought instant peace. Lulu returned in hang-dog fashion to her basket and the children made their way upstairs to the playroom.

It was gone half past seven when Harry appeared in his Rolls-Royce. He had dropped Len, his pianist, at the hall to try out the piano. David and Elspeth were transformed into a shy couple of innocents who had to be induced into an embrace with their larger-than-life uncle. Likewise, Mrs Cooper had to be propelled by Eleanor out of the kitchen and into the sitting room to meet my brother. She stood with her mouth wide open, speechless.

'Hello, love,' said my brother. 'How are you and how do you manage to cope with this lot? I think you deserve a medal.'

'Excuse me,' intervened Eleanor, 'I'm sure Mrs Cooper would find it much more of a handful if she had to look after your entourage!' That was the signal for our house-keeper to make a hasty withdrawal without saying a word.

'Sorry I frightened her,' replied Harry. 'I was only play-ing, honest.'

It took only half an hour or so to create an atmosphere in which even Mrs Cooper was made to feel at home. When the children were given presents of sweets and chocolates, their cup was running over. As we left for the Midnight Matinée, a blissful peace had descended upon the Vicarage.

At the Miners' Welfare Hall it was an entirely different scene. As soon as we entered the foyer my brother was besieged by a horde of autograph hunters. Backstage, the Abergelly Male Voice Choir were swarming around the corridors, resplendent in their sky-blue jackets and navy trousers, and all of them breathing out alcoholic fumes. Frank Wilson, the compère, was in Harry's dress-ing room checking on the details of his list of songs and arias. Through the open doors of the dressing room came the strains of the Four Rhythm Boys practising their contribution. Elizabeth Williams came to meet me in the corridor in a state of nervousness which bordered on mental collapse. 'Hold my hands, Vicar,' she pleaded, 'and please say a prayer for me.'

The only one who appeared to be unaffected by the occasion was Joe Williams, a veteran of Welsh variety. 'I've seen it all, Vicar,' he said, 'and tonight is just one more. Part of life's rich pageant.'

Graham Webb came to greet me just before he made his entrance to the podium in the hall. 'Don't worry,' he told me, 'I am sure tonight is going to be one of the best in Abergelly's entertainment history.'

As the programme got under way, the audience responded with increasing warmth to each item. By the time my brother appeared on the stage to the strains of 'I'm just wild about Harry', their applause was unrestrained. It took quite a while before he could announce that he was there because he had been commanded to do so by 'the black sheep of the family'. This was greeted by hysterical laughter. Every solo or aria was enough to raise the roof.

'And now,' he said, 'I should like to end this evening's performance with one of my favourite songs, "Bless this house".'

It took about three or four minutes before this announcement could subside into silence. His pianist played the opening bars. Suddenly, when it came to verse three, he forgot his words. We all looked at him and he looked at us. The Miners' Welfare Hall had never been so silent.

In a trice he became master of the situation. 'Shall we go back to verse one and retrace our steps?' he said. This time, he filled the hall with his magnificent voice in a faultless rendering of the old favourite.

Several minutes later, he made his way down to the dressing room. Outside was Ricky Palmer in his ankle-length coat and his bow tie. 'Sorry, Harry,' I said, 'but I promised this young chap that you could give him the name of an agent who could help him in show business.'

'Don't worry, Fred,' he said. 'This was me, fifteen years ago.'